The Avenue

The Avenue

DENNIS O'CONNELL

iUniverse, Inc.
Bloomington

The Avenue

iUniverse books may be ordered through booksellers or by contacting:

iUniverse
1663 Liberty Drive
Bloomington, IN 47403
www.iuniverse.com
1-800-Authors (1-800-288-4677)

ISBN: 978-1-4759-8862-8 (sc)
ISBN: 978-1-4759-8864-2 (hc)
ISBN: 978-1-4759-8863-5 (ebk)

Library of Congress Control Number: 2013908182

Printed in the United States of America

iUniverse rev. date: 05/17/2013

Acknowledgement

It would have been impossible for me to complete this book without the help of my friend and fellow author George Hess. His perseverance and patience allowed this book to become a reality. George is not just a friend. He is my mentor and teacher, and my life has become much richer for knowing him.

This one is for you, Tommy.
You will always be in our hearts.

TRIBALISM

: loyalty to a tribe or other social group especially when combined with strong negative feelings for people outside the group

The world that these young men knew was a world of tribalism with all the good and bad that comes with it—the fierce loyalty and the bitter rivalry, the blind trust and the violence borne of distrust.

Prologue

1977—July, The Bronx

Brother Martin made his way into the Sacristy and removed his robe from the closet containing vestments for the priest. As he slipped the garment over his head he noticed it was getting a little frayed where it touched the ground. He thought about replacing it but changed his mind, using the logic that it would be vain to change robes because of a small flaw. In truth he didn't change because the robe was soft and comfortable. He removed his street shoes, replacing them with his sandals.

He left the sacristy and made his way to Saint Anthony's Chapel. Dipping his fingers into the urns held by the two stone angels that bracketed the center aisle he made the sign of the cross with Holy Water.

He was a handsome man, tall with black hair streaked with gray. A member of the Capuchin Franciscan Friars, he was sworn to poverty, accepting nothing except to serve the church and Saint Frances.

Although only in his fifties he wore the demeanor of a man tortured. Darkness bracketed his eyes. His face held wrinkles born of years of agony.

He knew he was blessed by God to be allowed to serve in this beautiful church all these years. Father Martin was one of two priests serving this parish. The other seven clerics were Capuchin lay brothers. What he didn't understand was why God chose him to hear that tortured confession. Why he was selected by the Almighty to uncover the awful truth of that night after all these years?

Bound by his covenant with God he could not speak of what transpired in the confessional, but what was confessed to him was not the truth, although the penitent believed it happened the way it was told.

This torture would end tonight. He was leaving tomorrow, but before he was to leave he would unburden his secret to Father Jay in the confessional, before receiving the Sacrament. By not naming the penitent he would sidestep the vow of silence. He knew that without the penitent's permission he was in violation of the Seal of the Confessional, but he felt he had no choice. It was the only way he could share the agony that haunted him the last few days. The confession was made in error. That error needed to be corrected tonight, for he knew the truth, knew the destruction it would cause.

As he made his way to Saint Anthony's Chapel to hear his last confessions before retiring to the retreat in the Adirondack Mountains, he took note of the several parishioners waiting for him. He couldn't make out all their faces, as the light was poor in the chapel.

He entered the darkened confessional and closed the door behind him. He sat on the small bench, the mesh screen windows on each side of him. He would turn from one window upon completion of the confession and Act of Contrition, closing the sliding panel. He would then turn to the other window, sliding back the panel. He would then hear the confession of the waiting sinner. With the panel door open he began the sacrament.

He blessed the penitent and asked him to begin.

"Bless me Father for I am *about* to sin." Father Martin's head jerked up.

The soft whisper of the bullet passing through the silencer went undetected outside of the confessional. Father Martin's head fell forward, a small trickle of blood making its way from the hole in his temple. "Enjoy Heaven Father. You have earned it."

Chapter 1

1957—The Bronx,

"Boy, did they screw up this fuckin' map!" JP exclaimed.

"Yeh, look at the turf lines they drew for the Golden Guineas. It's all wrong," Mike piped in. The other three just nodded in agreement.

The object of their disapproval was a copy of the *Daily News*, New York's largest selling newspaper.

They were sitting at the soda counter in Slotnicks candy store, their chocolate egg creams pushed aside to make way for the newspaper that was opened to the centerfold. Slotnicks was a railroad car store, long and narrow. A glass counter on the left held a cash register and a box of assorted loose cigarettes on sale, two cents apiece. Inside the glass credenza was boxes of cigars. The wall, several feet in back of the credenza housed vertical slots holding packs of cigarettes. From the counter to the back of the store housed a long counter made of grey laminate, where sodas, ice cream and various refreshments were served. Eight stools were situated along the counter, with circular padded seats, their red linoleum covers cracked and patched through years of usage. On the right wall were racks of magazines, comic books and newspapers. The back wall contained two telephone booths.

Several of the stools were occupied by young gangbangers. Their attention was focused on a crudely drawn map of New York City. The map was divided into sections, each section labeled with the name of a youth gang or gangs that occupied that section. More than eighteen of these youth organizations occupied the page.

"They left out half the fuckin' gangs. Look at the territory they gave us. It's half the turf we roam." "I'm pissed!" Danny chimed in.

"That's fine with me," JP spoke. "We don't need the publicity. We got enough problems with the 47th Precinct. The last thing we need is those Irish bastards comin' down hard on us."

All four of the boys wore black shirts with a white boot of Italy patch over the left pocket. Their names were inscribed under the symbol. White lettering in script on the back of the shirts identified them as the Italian Berettas. They all wore jeans that sported hand rolled cuffs and all wore the familiar Ked sneakers. All the boys wore garrison belts. The one and a half inch leather belt fit neatly through the jean's belt loops. The edge of the buckle was sharpened and when used as a weapon could do as much damage as a stiletto.

This was the standard uniform of the day when just hanging around the Avenue.

"Boys! Do you mind moving outside and leave the newspaper here unless you pay for it! C'mon! move—move! You take up space, read my newspapers and comic books, and all you buy is a five-cent egg cream. Out!"

Aaron Slotnick was a short, bent over man who leased the small store pushing newspapers, candy, cigarettes and fountain drinks. He showed no fear of the tough street boys as he had faced much tougher adversaries in Auschwitz Concentration Camp during the war. Whenever the boys asked him about the number tattooed on his arm he ignored them.

"For Christ sake Aaron, we didn't finish our drinks—," Tony replied.

"As far as I'm concerned you're finished, you with your gangster shirts. Hoodlums! All of you! Those black shirts remind me of the Gestapo!"

"Yeah, but you love us old man."

"Out! Out!"

JP threw a quarter on the counter to pay for the drinks, and Danny paid him for the newspaper as they walked out the door. Although they had their arguments with the old man, the store was off limits. No trouble and no stealing. It was one of their hangouts, and Aaron accepted this and knew, if the boys wished, they could give him more grief than he needed. An easy truce existed between the Italian tough guys and the aged Jewish storekeeper.

This strange code held true for several of the establishments on White Plains Road or the "Avenue", the Bronx street they populated most days when not working or in school. The street ran north to south and was located in the Northeast section of the Bronx. Steel girders straddled the Avenue supporting the rails used by the Lexington Avenue Express. In this section of the Bronx the line was above ground and did not enter the tunnels of New York until it reached the lower Bronx. It was a lifeline for those commuters. They suffered through the heat, cold, and odors that came off their bodies, packed like sardines as they made their way back and forth to Manhattan to earn a living.

It was said if you didn't need a shower when you got on in the morning, you sure as hell needed one when you got off at night.

The corner of 225th Street and the Avenue housed the Park Hill, the local bar that served as a gathering place for the locals. Next door was a small TV repair shop. It was followed by Slotnicks candy store, John the Barber and Sharp's Liquors. The entrance to the subterranean pool hall and bowling alley followed. The local A&P Grocery Store stretched south to the corner of 224th Street. On the east side of the Avenue between 224th and 225th, the stores housed Father & Son shoes, the Blue Moon Bar and Grill, Renaldo's Bakery, and the local fish market.

The four boys were congregated in front of the candy store, conversation at a standstill for the moment as they waited for the northbound express to pull into the station. It was almost impossible to talk above the din caused by the hissing of air brakes and the screeching of the train coming to a stop. The slanting rays of sunlight that normally filtered through the gaps in the elevated line were temporarily blocked when the seven-car train pulled into the station. The noise and dust created by the behemoth was hardly noticed and taken in stride as it was a way of life accepted indifferently by the population which lived and worked in the area.

The boys paused in their newspaper reading as the throng of evening rush hour commuters made their way down the stairs from the train platform to the street. It was nearing 6:30 PM, the heat of the July day still reflecting in shimmering waves off asphalt sidewalks. Any chance of a breeze was blocked by the large steel structure, the stores that lined the Avenue, and the tenements that stretched along 224th and 225th Streets leading up to the Avenue.

"Look at the shines comin' off that train. You'd think this was Harlem, Goddamn it!" Tony spit in disgust.

Tony was Anthony Chicarella, tall and slightly overweight giving the impression of being muscular. He was eighteen years old and had a mean streak in him that constantly got him into trouble with the local authorities.

His family came over to America from Rimini, Italy, several years before he was born. His parents worked in the small bread and pastry shop they owned several blocks south on the Avenue. Tony kept his blonde hair long, combed into the style worn by most street kids—heavily pomaded and combed back into the pushed-in look of a ducks rear feathers. It was fondly called a "ducks ass" by those who sported the style. It was a standard hairdo among the gangs and helped define the look that identified them as gang members.

As most of the members were of Sicilian descent and were for the most part dark complexioned with black hair, Tony stood out like a neon light. His blue eyes and blonde hair made him a hit with the girls in the Sicilian neighborhood. He always bragged to the others of his "scores."

The other members of the gang had to constantly keep him in check to prevent him getting them into street fights they couldn't win. He had a festering hate for the blacks who he felt were invading the white territories of the Bronx, destroying the white man's way of life with their presence. He never hesitated to throw racial slurs at them or pick a fight as long as he thought he could win.

"Whoa! There's that chocolate honey goin' against the flow." Tony exclaimed, pointing to the black girl ascending the stairs to the train platform.

"She's probably headin' down to Harlem for the evening to see her honey!" Danny Marconi chipped in.

Danny Marconi, all five foot five inches of him, was typical Sicilian. Dark olive skin, brown eyes and black hair; he was a stereotypical southern Italian. He dropped out of school at sixteen, and for the two years following his departure he worked as a produce clerk in the local grocery store. He would be eighteen in two months and finally allowed to hang out in the Park Hill sucking on beers or a

Dewar's and soda. Danny was a follower and Tony was his role model. Anything Tony did was OK by him.

JP smiled. "I don't get it, Tony. For someone who hates anyone that's not a guinea you sure got a thing for colored girls."

Tony turned on him. "I don't wanna marry the bitch. I just wanna get a piece of it. Since when did you become a nigger lover?"

JP said nothing and went back to the newspaper, but there was tightness in his face. Although they grew up together there was always friction between them. JP was the undisputed leader of the Berettas and wore the mantle easily. Tony resented the fact he wasn't running the gang. He had more guts than JP, took more chances and wasn't afraid to mix it up with anyone. He was already being recruited by the local mob. They always could use another numbers runner, especially one with a temper and feared.

But when any decision had to be made regarding gang activities the other guys looked to JP.

Physically they were very different. Pascalli or "JP" as everyone called him was tall and lanky. His eyes bordered on black and his hair was the color of tar. He had the slightly hooked nose indigenous of Sicilian blood and his dark coloring gave the impression of a permanent tan. When he was angry his eyes seemed to get darker and his lips seemed to compress into his face. He feared little and where Tony showed his bravado in his loudness and being a bully, JP was quiet. Just his demeanor demanded respect. He was a natural leader. Although he graduated High School with grades that were not spectacular, it was not due to his intelligence as much as it was his lack of applying himself to his studies. However, graduating High School with an Academic Diploma was a feat in itself for these street kids.

Realizing it was foolish not to try to better himself in this neighborhood, he decided after registering for the draft that he would 'push his number', that is, ask to be drafted. In this way he would only serve two years, could pick his time to enter the Army and choose a career. He would do this at the end of summer. He realized that just hangin' on the Avenue and eventually become a numbers runner or shylock for the Anastasia family was a losing situation.

It was Anastasia's gopher Sally Guattro who came to JP and told him to cool the rising tension between the blacks and whites in the neighborhood. He told JP to rein in the Berettas and to tell the Shack Boys, the other youth gang that shared their turf, to do the same.

The black population was a lucrative business for the mob that supplied drugs and money to them. They used local black hoods to push the deadly highs in the Edenwald Projects, located several blocks east of the Avenue. It was the black pushers who went to Albert Anastasia asking him to reign in the young toughs so they could do their job. They didn't need the heat. Sally G was sending a message to JP, the Shack Boys, and the Club 22, the older gang that also shared the same turf that they had to back off the blacks. Business was too good.

JP wasn't stupid. The last thing he wanted was the colored coming at them from one side and the mob from the other. So he tried to reign in the gang and make them concentrate on more important things like making money. He always tried to defuse the tension between blacks and whites. Unfortunately he had a time bomb. Chicarella was constantly taunting the blacks that exited the station, and more than once fighting broke out between races because of his slurs. He particularly went after the black girl he called his "chocolate honey."

The young black girl was hot and absolutely beautiful. Her dark complexion, shapely body, and long black hair would turn any guy on. JP watched her walking up the stairs. In another world he would chase her, he mused. *Boy! What the hell would his girl think?*

The object of Tony's outburst was seventeen-year—old Cynthia Washington. She would catch the Lexington Avenue Express to 125th Street in Harlem where she would meet her cousin.

Cynthia moved to the Bronx from Harlem immediately after the Edenwald Projects were constructed. Subsidized by the state, the project offered low-cost housing for families in a low income bracket. The projects contained two and three bedroom apartments offering middle-class living in a safe rural neighborhood. Located one mile east of White Plains Road, it was necessary to take a bus from the Avenue to the Project entrance at Laconia Avenue. It was a small price to pay for living in the "country". People trapped in the crime-ridden Harlem community, situated in Manhattan, flocked to the State Housing Authority to apply for an apartment. As a result the mostly white community of the Northeast Bronx experienced a sudden influx of African Americans searching for a better life for their families.

Cynthia ignored the white guys standing around the entrance to the subway. Her mind was on upcoming dinner with her seventeen-year-old twin cousins Tanya and Peter and their five-year-old baby sister Alicia. Alicia was the love of the family. She was a precocious, gifted, and talented girl. She was also a beautiful child. However much her father and siblings loved her, the Washingtons loved her equally. She spent much of her free time in the projects with her cousins Cynthia, Louis, and her Uncle James. James worked nights, and on those days the Washingtons babysat her he would spend hours with her at the Bronx Zoo, the Botanical Gardens, and the movies. When it was time for him to go to work, he and Alicia rode the Lexington Avenue Express to Harlem where he would drop her off at her apartment before continuing on to his job. They would catch the 8:30 pm train at 225th Street and take it to 125th Street in Harlem. The engineer and conductor got to know her; they were impressed to where the engineer allowed them to join him in the engineer's booth. Alicia dazzled everyone who came into contact with her intelligence and wit. When she matured she would give her older sister strong competition. Cynthia missed Harlem. There was closeness in the community. Everyone knew one another; she could walk anywhere in the neighborhood that covered several square miles. She never felt threatened. These were her people; they loved and protected one another.

Even though the area was rife with crime, drugs, and robberies, she still felt safer in Harlem than the Bronx. The only difference was in the Bronx the bad guys were white, not black.

Cynthia was striking, with her slim neck and full lips. She had skin of ebony to go with a body of someone who exercised regularly. To JP there was no color, only beauty. To Tony it was just a black fantasy to screw.

Tony decided he would hang on the Avenue late tonight. He would watch for her coming off the train station. It was time she paid her dues. He would get Danny to hang with him.

Chapter 2

1957—The Bronx

They were sitting around the table in the restaurant area of the Pool room. It was used as a home base by the Berettas. Behind them the twelve bowling lanes were doing a brisk business. Off to their right the sixteen pool tables and two Billiard tables were getting maximum play also.

There were six Berettas and two Shack Boys gathered at the table. The Berettas totaled sixteen, the Shack boys eight. Missing were members of the third club that also lay claim to the Avenue, The 22 Socials. These were men in their early twenties, all Italian. They kept the peace in the neighborhood, sitting in on the younger club's war councils, advising them. Several of them were already soldiers in the Anastasia mob and any information, directions and orders that the mob wanted to impress on the Berettas and Shack Boys filtered down through the 22 Socials or Sally G. Such was the case this night.

One by one the remaining Berettas filtered in. Mike Scarpetta came down the stairs with Frankie Grazio. The clown of the gang Pete "Satch" Lombardo entered wearing his trademark baseball cap. The cap and his complexion likened him to the popular movie star Huntz Hall, consequently the name "Satch". With him was "Little Tom", whose actual name was Joe Rustico. He used the name when he boxed in the Golden Gloves, an event sponsored by PAL (Police Athletic League); he thought the name was more appealing than his own. With them was Gino Contelmo. Similar to all Sicilians

Gino was dark complexioned, short and stocky: his hair black and curly.

It was time to start the meeting. The sooner they finished the sooner they could get to the pool tables or to their girl friends waiting upstairs in Slotnick's.

Chapter 3

1957—The Bronx,

"Screw those white trash bastards. I think it's time we start hittin' back harder. I'm tired of those fuckers harassing our people. We have to stop takin' their shit."

The source of the anger was a boy by the name of Louis Washington. He was sitting at a table with six other youths in a room reserved for social affairs. Tonight it belonged to them.

The room was located in the heart of the Edenwald Projects. It was a large area with plenty of tables and chairs. Off to one side there was a kitchen complete with a refrigerator, stove and sink. The room was used for parties, social gatherings, dances; in this case a meeting of the Egyptian Kings, an offshoot group; part of the main organization that ran most of East Harlem.

"Be calm Louis. We'll get our turn. We're not strong enough to take on the Berettas, the Shack Boys and the 22 Socials at this time. They may harass us down on the Avenue but they won't step foot up here. Right now we play tit for tat. They do one of our people, we do one of theirs."

Eugene Montgomery was the oldest at eighteen, a tall strapping tough who unofficially ran the Bronx gang.

"We have to wait until we can get some help from the brothers downtown."

"That's all we do is wait. My sister can't walk on the Avenue without some white trash bastard making lewd remarks. She's frightened outta' her mind."

"Your sister would get comments from anyone regardless of color. In case you hadn't noticed she's a fox." Eugene replied. "If you weren't such an uptight bastard I would ask her out."

Louis gave Eugene an icy stare, and then broke out in a mirthless laugh. "Yeah, she's a fox and she's too good for you nigger. Don't let me catch you hounddoggin' her. You may think you're hot shit, but you ain't good enough for her!"

Eugene realized the conversation was getting tense. It was no secret that he had the hots for Louis's sister. He had time to win her over. She would belong to him regardless of Louis's feelings. He changed the subject.

"Our brothers' downtown just made an alliance with the Dragons on the east side to keep them off our back. Without worrying about the Dragons harassing us we can concentrate on bringin' together the brothers. We're already talkin' to the Mau-Mau's in Brooklyn. The Chaplins want a piece of these white boys also. Some of their members up here have had run-in's with the guineas. If we're goin' to take on the white boy's up here we're goin'to be needing a lot of firepower. We need help!"

"You tellin' me our boys made peace with that spic gang The Dragons?" The speaker was Claude Brown, a mean nasty street boy who would just as soon cut your throat as look at you. "It was those bastards that gave me this." The knife scar ran from his right ear down to his jawbone. It happened while locked up in the Tombs, the notorious jail in lower Manhattan; he was awaiting arraignment on a possessions charge. Unfortunately he was thrown into the general lockup with several of the Spanish Dragons, a rival gang. Thirty minutes later Brown was on his way to the Emergency room at Bellevue Hospital, his face slashed to the bone from a knife made from a piece of the bed spring in the cell. It was no comfort to Claude that one of the Dragons would carry a broken nose and another three missing teeth. In the two years since the incident his hate for them never abated. It was no secret that he had put two more of them in the hospital since, laying in wait for them with a baseball bat. The Dragons had no love for him either.

"That's right Claude,' Eugene countered. "And part of the agreement is that we reign you in. You listenin'?"

"I hate these white boys almost as much as I hate the Dragons, but I'll back off temporarily. You tell them they're safe for the time being'."

Eugene continued. "The white boys are in disarray. The Berettas, the Golden Guineas, the Daggers are beatin' up on one another over turf issues and their women. The Club 22 boys think it's just kid stuff and won't get involved. By the time they realize who's runnin' things up here it will be too late. We'll control the North Bronx, an' it'll be their women who will be afraid to walk the streets."

Louis pushed the chair back and stood. "If this meeting is over I would like to go home and see my family; besides my cousins are visiting. I would like to see them before they have to leave to catch the 8:30 express."

Chapter 4

1957—The Avenue

The heat was stifling. Although it was almost 10 pm there was no letup. During the day the concrete absorbed the rays of the sun; at night the sidewalks and blacktopped streets poured the heat back into the air. There was no breeze. The tenements and elevated subway structures assured there would be none.

The Avenue was alive with movement. Escaping the heat of closed-in apartments with no air conditioning the tenants took to the streets in search of any semblance of a breeze. The street corners bisecting the Avenue were meeting places for all types and ages. Several Berettas were gathered at the corner of 225th Street and the Avenue, along with a few of the Shack Boys. Off to the side several girls were chatting among themselves discussing the Immaculate Conception Church dance scheduled for the upcoming weekend.

Under the elevated tracks vehicular traffic was flowing freely north and south; headlights from the cars casting long shadows on the steel girders supporting the rails. Between the steel girders and the sidewalk, cars were parked and double-parked, the owners either in the local bar, the poolroom or just hanging about. Trolley cars passed infrequently under the steel structure on tracks molded into the blacktop and cobblestone road. Discharging and boarding passengers on even numbered street corners, the clanging bell warning riders the trolley was about to depart. Occasionally the noise level was raised as the Lexington Avenue Express made its presence known pulling in and out of the 225th Street station. It was as if the Avenue itself was a living breathing entity thriving on the energy of its inhabitants.

JP was off to the side leaning on one of the parked cars, his arms around the waist of a petite brunette. Her hair was tied back into a ponytail. She wore a white, sleeveless low-cut blouse tucked into a pair of red pedal pushers. The pink lipstick she wore accentuated her olive skin. Her name was Teresa Schiavone. She was JP's present girlfriend.

"You're awful quiet JP. What's going on in that little mind of yours?"

"I wonder where Tony and Danny are. They're usually around."

"I'm sure they're into some scam. I saw them in Tony's car heading up towards Bronxwood Avenue when I was comin' up here. I gave them a shout, but I guess they didn't hear me."

"Now, why the hell would they be headin' up that way? The only thing up there is trouble."

"I'm getting jealous. Your thoughts should be on me and how you're gonna make me happy tonight. Forget those two slugs."

"Yeah, right. Let's check and see who wants to ride out to City Island for clams. Maybe it's a little cooler out there."

But even as he was talking, his focus was on the stairs leading up to the train station. He spotted her a few minutes after the express pulled into the station. She was making her way down the stairs, oblivious to her surroundings. JP's eyes wandered towards the bus stop. Due to the Bus companies cutting the nighttime schedules there was no vehicle presently at the bus stop.

Terri wandered over to the rest of the group to try to get a few of them to move towards their cars. JP watched the young black girl walk past the bus stop and make her way east towards the projects. He had a lousy feeling about this and couldn't shake his sense of foreboding. As the influx of families moving to the Bronx from the other boroughs increased so did the numbers of young people. The Egyptian Kings were getting stronger as more and more teenagers relocated from Manhattan and Brooklyn were recruited into their ranks. It wouldn't take much to ignite a full scale race war.

Push it from your mind *asshole!* He thought. You have better things to think of, like where's my girl? JP turned towards the group. "Let's get outta here. I got a willy for some clams on the half shell!"

Chapter 5

1957—The Avenue

"Tony, what the fuck are we doin' parked here? She's goin' to jump on the bus. How do you know she's even coming back here? Maybe she's staying in Manhattan for the night. We're wasting our time."

The 1951 yellow-and-black Buick Roadmaster they were sitting in stood out like a neon light.

"I just have a hunch Danny. The bus schedule is cut way back this time of night. She'll walk home rather than wait at the bus stop. Another half hour, ok?"

They were parked on the south side of 225th Street near Barnes Avenue, one street up from the Avenue. It was on the bus route to Laconia Avenue and the Projects. When the buses weren't running or were late, the alternative was a half-hour walk to the projects.

They sat in the car, their cigarettes giving off a soft glow in the darkness. The humidity hung like a heavy blanket over the city. There was not a breeze in the air. They were perspiring profusely as the heat in the car continued to rise. The few people passing the parked car averted their eyes and walked a little faster.

Tony was keeping an eye on the rear view mirror when he spotted her making her way up the sidewalk. There were no other pedestrians in sight.

"There she is Danny! I knew we would get lucky."

Danny's features were contorted in fear. "We're not gonna hurt her are we, Tony?"

"Na. We'll just give her a taste of bein' with a white man. She'll never want to go back to her nigger friends again."

15

Cynthia was lost in thought. She had had a wonderful time with her family. Alicia was a trip. At five years old she had the mind of a teenager. She was already in the second grade, skipping kindergarten and the first grade. She was brilliant, yet she had all those five year old traits that endeared her to her family. Cynthia looked forward to Alicia's visits to the Bronx and staying over with Cynthia and her family. Cynthia's father adored Alicia and she in turn loved being with them. With Peter and Tanya always busy, and her father working all day, she looked forward to spending days at a time at the Washingtons apartment in the Bronx with her cousins and uncle.

No matter how dirty Harlem was, regardless of the bad reputation of the area, Cynthia always felt comfortable among her own people. Aside from a few whistles and hoots, she was left alone. She missed her teenage friends and family from the close knit Harlem community.

She heard the car door open and saw the interior dome light of the car illuminate the occupants. Her features contorted into a mask of fear. She started to run but was cut off by the taller of the two. The strength of his grasp spun her around and she fell to her knees. She tried to scream but his right arm encircled her head while his left was around her waist. She reached behind her, arms flailing. She touched skin raking her nails across the assailants face. He screamed in pain as he dragged her to the open door of the car and forced her into the back seat. Her head hit the roof of the car dazing her. He climbed in pressing his body on top of her to stop her struggling. Blood was streaming down his face caused by the deep scratches.

"You bitch!" He punched blindly catching her in the forehead with his fist.

"Move it Danny. Get this fuckin' car outta here.

Chapter 6

1977—Manhattan, New York

She ached all over. After five hours of shooting, the pain in back of her eyes came like flashes of light. *Enough*!

"I need a break Tommy."

"Two more sequences Tanya, and then we'll call it a day."

She was in the shower two hours later, her arms straight out in front of her as if holding up the wall. Her eyes were shut as she allowed the scalding water to cascade down her body. She was exhausted. Where was the glamour now?

She stepped out of the shower and began drying herself. Standing in front of the full-length mirror she paused to appraise herself. She was pleased with the reflection. A product of an oriental mother and an African-American father, she possessed the best of both parents. Her beauty was radiating. She wore her hair long, allowing it to tumble around her shoulders. Her figure was flawless, on the slim side accentuating her breasts; though she felt they could have been smaller. Her face was oriental with thin lips and eyes that were slightly slanted, a trait from her mother. Her eyes were gray-green, luminous in the light. They were hypnotizing, and it sometimes embarrassed her when she caught someone staring at her. She realized that even her beauty would someday fade condemning her to the legions of has-beens that existed in her profession.

At thirty seven years old she was still among the highest—paid models in the world. There wasn't a day that went by that her photograph didn't adorn the cover of some magazine or tabloid. She slipped into her satin robe and walked barefoot into the kitchen. After pouring herself a glass of chilled wine, she walked into the den and sat at her desk, finally getting an opportunity to browse through the Wall Street Journal and the New York Times. Louisa, her maid, made sure the latest copies of the two newspapers were on her desk every day. Tanya flicked through the Wall Street Journal to the stock market results. A small smile played on her face as she noted that TR, Inc. was up two points. She had opened four new stores over the weekend, two of them in France. The Tanya Reinford line of Lingerie and nightwear was sold the world over at ridiculously high prices, catering to the more affluent clientele.

Supermodels adorned the pages of her lingerie calendar, and her TV ads bordered on being risqué.

She picked up the latest copy of *Business Week*, her face adorning the cover under the caption **"Supermodel, Super Salesperson, and Super Rich—Tanya Reinford. One of the Fortune 500"**. The ringing of the phone interrupted her thoughts. She was going to let the phone go to the answering machine until she recognized the caller

"Hi Peter, how's my favorite older brother

Making money for me and keeping me honest?"

Her favorite brother was Peter Reinford, older by 3 minutes. He was an identical twin, and he was described not as handsome but beautiful, having the same features, coloring and traits as his sister.

Both graduated from the Sorbonne in Paris France. Both came back to America to obtain their masters degree. Peter joined Ford Motors after Graduation. In less than three years he progressed to CFO of Automotive International under Lee Iacocca. When his sister asked him to become her business manager for TR International he jumped at the chance. In the business world it was rumored they could read each other's min; they were that similar.

"Read today's *Daily News* beautiful?"

"Didn't get past the Stock Market in the Journal, and you know I don't read the *Daily News*."

"How's this for a headline.

"PRIEST MURDERED WHILE HEARING CONFESSIONS"

"That's terrible but why is that supposed to interest me big brother?"

"His name was Father Martin."

He heard her sharp intake but the silence was louder. Finally she spoke. "Dear God, he was a good man. Who would do such a thing? Do they have any suspects?"

"Don't know. Sis, if they do they're not talking. I'll be flying back today. I bet you didn't know they sold the *Daily News* in France. Can I take you to dinner tonight? I would rather you not roam that six room condo all night.

You gotta get a guy and get married!"

"I tried it once. It didn't work. Call me when you get in. If I'm still conscious we'll do something."

"Congratulations on the *Business Week* cover. You made the top five hundred."

"And still climbing, dear brother."

"Pick up a copy of the magazine, Sis. You might want to browse through the Five Hundred richest."

"OK. Whose name am I looking for?"

"I don't think I'll tell you. Might ruin your day altogether, or maybe it might make your day. By the way, Sammy Davis hitched a ride from Paris on our Lear. He will be in New York For a stint at the Copa; wants to have dinner if you're available. See ya' later."

Tanya picked up the copy of *Business Week* and made her way out to the terrace.

A slight breeze was blowing from the north, the coolness caressing her warm skin. The view was spectacular. The west side of Manhattan lay before her sparkling in the night. Far below, the slow moving traffic reminded her of giant snakes winding their way through the streets of New York. She was far removed from the noise of blaring horns and the hustle of thousands of New Yorkers making their way home.

She sat and began perusing the article, immediately spotting her company listed 349th in the list, her name appearing as CEO of TR, Inc. She smiled to herself, knowing that next year's issue of *Business Week's* Fortune 500 would find her much higher on the coveted list of multi-millionaires. As she perused the list, her eyes locked in on the name associated with Starchip Enterprises, currently 330th on the list and, according to the short biography, rapidly climbing. The company specialized in microchip technology, and its latest breakthrough was poised to revolutionize the Computer industry. Tanya continued to stare at the name of the founder and current CEO of the company. She dropped the paper, her eyes welling up. The tears were coming freely now, and she found it hard to breathe. All these years, she thought. I blocked him out all these years! She tried to stop the memories as they flooded her senses. What about him? He must know what I have achieved. Is he reacting the same way I am? What is going on in his mind? Does my name in print or my photo shoots bring back to him the nightmare of that summer? Does he relive the pain and suffering as I have? What would happen if his past was exposed to those who pass judgment today? She lay back on the couch and folded herself into a fetal position allowing the memories to flow through, forcing her to relive that summer.

Chapter 7

1957—The Avenue

JP was sitting at the counter in Slotnicks sucking on a chocolate egg cream. Del walked in and sat next to him.

"Hey, Del."

"Hey, JP. What's up?"

"Where the fuck you been?"

"Miss me, eh? Better w—watch out. P—P-People will talk"

John Delgardo's parents came from a town north of Naples, Italy. He was dark skinned but his features were Northern Italian. He was very quiet partly due to a stuttering problem acquired during a bout with rheumatic fever when he was a child. Del's affliction was off limits. If anyone teased him they would find themselves flat on their ass. Even Tony gave him some space. The only person allowed to rib him was JP. They were that close. He also was going in the Army at the end of the summer. "I w-was up the county, Mahopac.

W-What's goin'on?"

"We got the word from Sally G. Lay off the blacks. We're hurting the drug trade, and the numbers take is down.

"I'm worried about Tony and Danny."

"Haven't them since yesterday, and I get the feeling' they're up to no good. They fuck with the niggers, Anastasia's boys are goin' to come down on us. The Socials also told us to back off. Gino Paparazzi, their President let me know in no uncertain terms that we are to cool it"

"So, w-what's the p-problem? T-Tell T-Tony to b-back off. You w-want me t-to t-talk t-to him?"

JP had a smile on his face. "Well let's see. I'm five foot eight and your five foot ten. Tony's five eight. Think we can reign him in?"

"I'll talk to him, JP. Now, what's your Mom cooking? I'm hungry. Today's Friday. Gotta be Baccala."

"You notice Del, that when it comes to talking' about food you don't stutter?"

"Fuck you, JP. Let's go eat"

Walking through the Italian neighborhood, the rich odors of fish, and tomato sauce cooking assaulted the senses. It was Friday and according to Catholic Doctrine, a meatless day. tomato sauce marinara, homemade pizza, pasta sarde finocchio, made from sardines and fennel. The overpowering aroma of dried salted cod baking after soaking for twenty-four hours overpowered the squalid smell of the streets. It was this pungent aroma of Baccala that caused JP and Del to quicken their step.

"Hey, Wait for me. I knew you guys were going to grandpa's house."

"Mike, you're another one. You smell food and you're like a leach. C'mon. Good thing my mom loves you. You're the standard for all of us."

Mike Scarpetta was tall, dark, with black hair combed into the proverbially ducks-ass. He was on his way, the token guinea in the world of investment. He was heading for Yale with a 3.9 average. His ethnic background and smooth talking guaranteed him a position with one of the more prestigious investment firms. Only his fellow Berettas' knew that he possessed a nasty streak that blossomed when he was hitting on an adversary. He hated black people and too many times he teamed up with Tony to cave some Negro's head into the ground. However, around people who might help him he was a sweetheart, and his friend's families adored him.

The street where JP's family lived ran parallel to the Avenue and one street west. It was immaculate. There were no newspapers, garbage or detritus in the streets. The sidewalks were swept, the garbage collected and placed into bags for the garbage trucks to collect. The two and three story homes stood side by side with narrow driveways between them that led to backyards that boasted of tomato plants, fig trees and grape arbors.

The street was alive with activity. A few of the younger kids were playing stickball to pass the time until supper. People were sitting outside their homes on their porch steps trying to escape the stifling heat inside. Radios by their sides blasted out the Yankee—Red Sox game. There were six or seven people sitting on folding chairs and on the front steps to JP's grandfather's house listening to the game.

JP's mother had moved in to care for her father and lived on the first floor to be near him. JP's cousin Nancy and her husband with their two children rented the second floor apartment, and JP would occupy the attic until he left for the Army.

JP and the two boys passed through the gate saying their hello's as they entered the house. If anyone was surprised there were two more mouths to feed, they hid it well. His cousin Louie raised his head from under the hood of his '55 Ford. "You punks want a beer, they're in the cooler. If you drink more than one each you buy some more. Capisce?"

JP nodded to him. "Thanks cuz. We'll say our hellos inside and be right out. Make some room on the steps."

The house was as hot as a furnace, but no one seemed to mind. The three boys made their way into the kitchen where three women were bustling about getting ready for dinner. "Got two more refugees Mom."

JP's mom turned from the stove, the perspiration streaming down her face kept at bay by a wet towel. JP kissed his Mom and said hello to her two sisters who were setting the table. All nodded hello. JP's mom set two more places at the twelve-foot table that dominated the room.

Seated at one end of the table was the head of the household, Peter Marcone, giving orders to his three daughters. He was an imposing figure. At eighty-five years old he stood six foot four weighing almost three hundred pounds. Born in Sicily, he and his brothers came over to the United States with their parents in the late 1800's as immigrants settling in the Bronx. They opened a leather goods factory and store in Manhattan that grew into a profitable business. He and his wife raised nine children. His wife had passed away several years ago. To date he counted twenty-seven grandchildren.

After dinner they sat around the table picking on fruit and cheese. The bottle of anisette was on the table to accompany the cups of demitasse.

JP turned to his grandfather. "Pop, how's everything at the Sons of Italy Club? Playing a lot of Bocce?"

"If you stop by once in a while you could play some with us. But you too busy tryin' to be a tough guy." He talked with the guttural dialect of a Sicilian invading his broken English. "You wear those black shirts. You bring a bad name to the Italians."

"It brings us respect, Pop. We need to band together, what with the blacks moving up invading our neighborhoods."

"You think you're goin' to stop this incursion? They are trying to find a better life away from the dirt of Harlem."

"They bring the dirt here. Let them stay up in the projects and off the Avenue."

"He's right Pop," his son Peter Jr. spoke. They come up here and they have no respect. They're no good thieves and troublemakers, most of them on welfare. They pass smart remarks to our young women. The stores on the Avenue have installed gates across their doors because of those pigs. They should go back to Harlem. The streets are not safe anymore"

"You hear what my son says, JP? I tried not to teach my children hate, but obviously I have failed. I understand when the blacks exit the train subway station they are in fear because of you and your friends hanging around the train station. I remember when your father was alive and he preached how much better you were than the blacks. Are you going to preach that to your children? Are you going to tell your children how Anastasia and his Mafioso thugs supply the drugs to those who need a fix? That he is the real enemy, and not some poor black trying to better himself. Contrary to what my son says, the neighborhood is changing and we need to adapt to those changes, not fight them.

"The blacks are a minority now, but that will change and the day will come when they will be looking down their noses at some other group; they will flex their muscles like you are flexing yours today. It is a pecking order. Some group must always be on the bottom. First it was the Irish, then the Italians and now the blacks. Who can say what group will be relegated to the bottom next. Perhaps the Puerto Ricans."

"That ain't goin to happen, Pop. Not as long as we stick together."

"But you will not be here, JP. You will be gone the end of the summer, won't you? Maybe the Army will change your outlook and make you more tolerant. Maybe, just maybe, you and your friend Del will not permanently inherit the sins of your fathers."

Chapter 8

1957—The Bronx

Fordham Hospital, located in the South Bronx just north of The Bronx Zoo, turned no one away. Running a close second to Bellevue Hospital in Manhattan, they handled the bulk of beaten, shot, raped, abused and accident victims north of 138th street.

The two paramedics catching a smoke outside the emergency room watched with curiosity as the big Buick pulled into the driveway, the passenger side door partially open. They did react when the body tumbled to the pavement as the car pulled away without stopping. Concentrating on the still figure in the road, neither man caught the license plate number of the car. Kneeling next to the girl, one of the men felt for a pulse. Feeling one, he yelled for a stretcher. Five minutes later, after stabilizing her, Cynthia Washington was on her way to the OR, the code for the neurosurgeon on call to report 'stat'.

Hours later she was in the Intensive care unit in a coma, her arm in a cast, her head wrapped in bandages, and her eyes swollen shut. Apparently the fall from the car caused a trauma to her brain. If she recovered she would carry a large scar on the right side of her head where surgery had to be performed to relieve the pressure of her brain swelling. She was listed as Jane Doe as she had no identification on her person. Her identification would have to wait until she came out of the coma. If she passed away she would just be another casualty for potter's field.

Two policemen interviewed the paramedics. All they could remember was that it was a big car, paint job yellow and black. They did not get a good look at the occupants or the license plates. The cops folded their notebooks and left. If she passed away the case would be given to Homicide. It would be added to the mountain of unsolved crimes that would eventually go into the cold case files. A black kid beaten and raped in the South Bronx did not garner much attention.

What the police didn't count on was the dedication and skill of the attending physicians and the victim's will to live. She was no quitter. What the police and the physicians couldn't know was that she would awake from the coma on a slow news day. She would tell her story and set off a chain of events that would have a major impact on life in the North Bronx.

Chapter 9

1977—New Orleans

The heat was stifling; the humidity as high as it could go without raining. The crowds were large; the stink from the littered streets giving off an odor of dead fish and unwashed bodies. This certainly was not in the brochure, he thought as he bar hopped down Bourbon Street. He spent little time on the street itself opting for air-conditioned bars with their tourists, con artists, and prostitutes.

He walked into Larry Flint's Hustler Club and found a small table near the stage. A topless dancer with the name of Honey Pot was gyrating on the stage and was in the process of removing her G-string, baring all. Now, this he liked. The topless waitress came over and took his order for a Dewar's and soda at five dollars a pop. He didn't care. He was flush, and there was plenty more where that came from. Being a pit boss in Vegas had its perks, one being healthy kickbacks from the dealers.

As he was enjoying his fourth scotch, the woman he chose to bed down with that night sat across from him. She was tiny without being too thin. She had the soft features of a teenager and wore no makeup, her hair tied in a ponytail. The way he was eyeballing her, she knew he was into young girls. She was twenty-two but looked fifteen. She was never without customers.

"How about a lap dance, mister. Only ten bucks?"

"Skip the dance. How would you like to make a couple of hundred?"

"I get off at one. I'll meet you down the street at Hemingway's. It'll cost you two hundred plus the room. You still have to take the lap dance; and no, I'm not going back to *your* room"

"No problem."

Four hours later she gathered her clothes and started getting dressed.

"Why don't you stay the night, sugar? I got the bread."

"I've got another appointment darlin'; but thanks. You paid for the room so leave whenever you feel like. Come by and see me again. After all, better me than a real fifteen year old," she said sarcastically as she left.

Fuck her, he thought. Just because I like them young don't mean I'm a pedophile.

There was a knock on the door. She's back, the bitch! She'll really earn her money this time. "Comin', sugar." He got up and padded to the door. "Welcome back". He opened the door. "I know you—. Who the hell—?" Before he could react he felt the sharp pain of the knife slip into his stomach. He slid to the floor trying to stem the flow of blood streaming from his body. He lay there staring. "Why?"

"That's for 1957. The Avenue! Look at me!"

"No! No!" he whispered as his life ebbed out of him. His last thoughts were of the Bronx and 1957.

Joe Rustico, aka Little Tom, lay dead in a sleazy hotel room, finally understanding.

Chapter 10

1977—Manhattan

Peter walked into the small Chinese restaurant located on Mott Street in lower Manhattan. It was definitely not a tourist attraction. The small sign over the blackened windows of the storefront gave the impression of a rundown eatery guaranteeing ptomaine poisoning to anyone who had the courage to sample its wares.

Upon entering the restaurant, however, the atmosphere changed drastically. There were twelve booths along one wall. Opposite each booth a tapestry hung, each one containing a symbol representing the Chinese calendar, intricately woven into the fabric. Small overhead fans whispered above the soft sound of central air conditioning. At the front of the store was a small concierge desk. The odor of Chinese herbs and sauces wafted into the room from the rear.

Five of the booths were occupied; the patrons well dressed Chinese, with the exception of one booth.

"Good evening Mr. Reinford, your sister is waiting for you." The young Chinese girl at the desk escorted Peter to the last booth.

"Hi, Sis." He sat opposite her, kissing her on the cheek. If anyone in the restaurant recognized them it was not acknowledged. It would be insulting. The young Chinese waiter appeared, and they ordered drinks. They waited until he returned from the rear with their order. There was no menu given. The waiter informed of the available selections for that evening, took their order and left.

"You sounded kind of shook up when I talked to you earlier, Sis. It still haunts you that much?"

"After twenty years I still haven't been able to stop the nightmares, Peter. I cannot sleep nights thinking of what I did. Reading his name and seeing his face in *Business Week* just exacerbated the horrible dreams."

"It was not your fault. Not in the least. You have to stop doing this to yourself."

"Peter I won't feel better until I know they get what's coming to them. But I was just as bad as they were, and I can never forgive myself or them. They deserve the worst kind of misery. Unfortunately, I'm as guilty as they are."

"Stop talking like that. You're rich, famous and at the risk of being conceited, you're beautiful. You have the world. You are involved in more charities and programs to help young black kids than any other celebrity. You're a heroine in the eyes of the Black Community."

"If they knew what happened in the Bronx twenty years ago they would despise me."

"They don't know and they will never know what happened. I will promise you that much. Here comes our food. Let's enjoy it and talk about some positive things like our new outlets in France."

"While I'm in town I would like you and I to go up to Harlem tomorrow to see Cynthia. We haven't seen her in months." Tanya offered.

"How is she doing?"

"I believe a lot better than I am. She also called me earlier. She read the story relating to Father Martin's death."

"What was her reaction?"

"She was saddened by his death. Although his name brought back terrible memories of the Bronx, she always felt that Father Martin was one of the good guys. She felt his death was related to those horrible days in 1957."

"How can that be? Who could want him dead? All he ever did was attempt to bring the races together. He treated us like humans."

"I don't know Peter, but I agree with Cynthia. I have a horrible feeling about the way he died."

Chapter 11

1977—The Bronx

Lieutenant Billy Mongelli sat in his office with his feet perched comfortably on the desk. He was eating a cream-filled donut that naturally went with the unending coffee he consumed.

He watched the hustle and controlled chaos around him as the flow of humanity moved through the 47th Precinct. Sited on Laconia Avenue in the Edenwald projects, the precinct had the highest crime rate in Bronx County. The holding cells did a booming business temporarily housing druggies, felons, whores, and gangbangers until they could be moved.

Who would believe that I missed the old building with its cadre of Irish police, Mongelli mused. The structure he was referring to was the old 47th Precinct between 229th Street and 230th Street fronting the Avenue. The red brick façade on the building was streaked gray with time. The detritus from the streets, cars, and subway clung to the building like a shabby old coat. The inside of the building wasn't any better. The smell of cigarettes, cigars, unwashed bodies, and backed up toilets left a permanent odor that was indescribable. The two-story building had been home to 60 patrolmen and several detectives of various ranks.

The building finally closed down in 1972. It was declared unsafe and hazardous; the final nail being a tanker carrying fuel oil that lost control and put an eighteen-foot hole in the front of the building.

Well, I won't miss this rat hole ether, Billy thought. In approximately one month I'm out of here, with twenty-five years on the job. He looked around him. Sure would like to know who decided all police station walls should be painted shit green. Been lookin' at those colors for twenty-five years. Now I know why so many cops eat their guns.

Twenty-five years ago he started in the 47th as a foot patrolman. He was not only the shortest guy in the precinct but the only Italian among all the Irish. At five foot six he was built like a fireplug. Except for the crows feet around his eyes and the slight graying at his temples, he was in remarkable shape for his age. He had a reputation of being tough but fair and was well liked by his peers.

It was thought he would make a difference and could communicate with the mostly Italian residents. It turned out to be a real joke. Like any other cop in the neighborhood he was reviled. The only communication he had with them was with the end of his lead-filled nightstick.

Now look at the neighborhood, he thought. What a melting pot. Blacks, Puerto Ricans, Asians, and even some die hard whites made up the population. The precinct was seventy-five percent black to accommodate the majority of residents. Twenty-five years ago you could count the number of black families on one hand. Times sure have changed since that summer.

He heaved a sigh and picked up the *Daily News*, leafing through the pages. He perused the lead story in the paper.

Priest Murdered While Hearing Confessions

Mongelli put the paper down, not realizing he was rubbing the old gunshot wound on his left thigh. Son of a bitch, he whispered. Talk about what goes around comes around. I wonder if the priest's last thought was of that night twenty years ago.

His thoughts drifted back. He could almost hear the sound of the Lexington Avenue Express rumbling by above his head. Over the years the recurring sound of the train as it passed, was a small certainty in his life, and the recurring din was actually comforting.

Chapter 12

1957—The Bronx

The music was loud, blasting its way into the street outside the church. It was Friday night and the Franciscan Friars who cared for the beautiful church opened its doors to the young.

Immaculate Conception Church was located on Gun Hill Road (210th Street) less than a quarter mile east of the Avenue. Built in 1903, it was a masterpiece of architecture inside and out. Its majestic twin spires seemed to symbolize the power of the church. Inside, the magnificent sculptures of Saint Ann, the Virgin Mother, and Saint Joseph dominated the altar. The huge stained glass window suffused the interior of the church with a soft light. High above, looking down on the parishioners were paintings on the domed ceiling depicting scenes from the New and The Old Testaments.

However, the doors the Franciscan Friars opened to teenagers were not to the church but to the gym inside the school. The brothers supplied a DJ (one of their own), light refreshments and food. All teenagers were welcome to eat, drink, dance, and hang out until 10:30pm.

There were a few rules that friars laid down. No gang shirts or gang colors allowed, and no smoking in the building. All races and creeds were allowed to attend the dance. The church and school grounds were neutral zones. The slightest threat of an altercation between groups would mean expulsion from the dance for the instigating party. If the incident was serious enough they would not be allowed back for future gatherings.

Most of the Franciscan Friars were young men in their late twenties and thirties. When their duties permitted they exercised, played basketball, and took to swimming in the Olympic sized pool on the grounds. The long brown robes they wore did little to hamper their movements on the basketball court. At every dance there were at least four friars acting as chaperones. They didn't hesitate to whack a teenager who got out of line, or throw him out. Aside from the friars there were at least two police cruisers parked in front of the church and four foot patrolmen mingling with the sixty plus teenagers who attended the dance. Because most of the Police were good Irish Catholics, they tolerated these dances. However, in their eyes, these gatherings were powder kegs ready to blow at any time. If they saw someone out of line they didn't hesitate to use their lead filled nightsticks to bring the perpetrator to the floor with a sharp crack across the back of his knees.

This Friday night the gym was crowded. Although the temperatures hovered in eighties it didn't stop the frenzied gyrations of the dancers as they danced to "Jailhouse Rock"; everyone was having a great time.

Most of the gangs were represented. The Fordham Daggers, the Golden Guineas, the Shack Boys and the Berettas came in force. Although they all had their problems with one another, they were on their best behavior under the watchful eyes of the friars and cops. Most of their troubles centered on the girls attached to the various gangs. Unless they had permission, a girl attached to one gang did not associate with a guy from another gang.

The record changed and the voice of Pat Boone singing "April Love" filled the gym. Little Tom, his eye on one of the Dagger Debs, left the Berettas and walked over to where the Daggers were milling around. He asked Tommy G, the leader of the group if it was ok to dance with one of the Dagger Debs. She wasn't attached to any one guy, so he was given the nod. He walked over to her and started handing her a line as to why she should dance with him, when peripherally he saw the group entering the gym. The cacophony of sounds emanating from the dozens of teenagers dropped to a whisper. Two of the patrolmen stationed themselves inside the door next to Officer Mongelli as Louis Washington and his crew entered the building. Four girls and six guys made their way to an empty corner of the gym and milled around. Little Tom couldn't help but notice the look of fear on Danny's face when the black teenagers entered the gym. He turned to Grazio, one of the other Berettas. "You see the look in Danny's eyes. He looks frightened."

"Yeah, like a deer in the headlights of a car."

A few of the blacks went over to the refreshment stand and retrieved sodas and franks, ignoring the hard stares they received from the whites across the room. JP, dancing with Terri ignored the tense atmosphere created by the entrance of the Egyptian Kings.

"In case you hadn't noticed, JP. We got company, and I do believe they're black," Terri whispered in his ear.

"Yeah, it's a great country, darlin'; there's a first for everything. Kinda balsy of them, though." She smiled at JP. "Well, the church doesn't discriminate. Here comes Father Martin to greet our new guests."

The song ended and the gym started rocking to the sound of Little Richard singing "Lucille."

Father Martin walked over to Washington, "Welcome to our church dance. It's always nice to see new young people here."

Washington smiled at him. "I noticed the welcoming committee at the door;" he nodded towards the three police officers carrying their nightsticks at their side.

"Please," Father Martin countered, "You're welcome and enjoy yourselves."

Louis Washington and Eugene Montgomery took two of the girls on the floor to dance. The tension seemed to ease some as the dance floor became crowded with the young dancers.

JP was standing by the refreshment table watching Washington dance, except his eyes weren't on Washington but the girl he was dancing with. She was beautiful. Dressed in Jeans and sneakers and a see through-peasant blouse, she took his breath away. Her long hair came down to her shoulders and glistened against her light chocolate skin. She had an oriental look about her, and JP guessed she was of mixed blood. All he could think of was she had inherited the best of both worlds.

He received a poke in the ribs. "You keep staring like that and you're going to trip over your tongue, big guy."

"C'mon, Terri. Let's dance."

"Since when you interested in black girls?"

"Don't break my balls. I'm only interested in you, darlin'"

"You better be, or I'll cut those balls off."

Officer Mongelli and his colleagues were posted just inside the door watching the gyrating teens; a worried look creased his face. Father Martin walked to him.

"You have a concerned look on your face, Officer Mongelli. Besides the normal concerns about bringing this melting pot together, what's troubling you?"

"Aren't you concerned that this could blow up any moment, Father?"

"I know of no other way to bring them together, to show that they are very much alike regardless of the color of their skin. But that's not what is troubling you, is it, Officer?"

"Something is off kilter here, Father, but I can't put my finger on it."

"If it brings you consolation, Officer, I feel the same way. The boys from Edenwald projects seem subdued, unusually quiet."

Although Officer Mongelli was in uniform and carrying a weapon, he was not officially on duty. Like many of his colleagues, he made extra money moonlighting as a security officer when it didn't interfere with his occupation as a police officer. He was paid by the church to keep the peace at various events, and, although it was not sanctioned by the police force they overlooked his need to earn additional money.

Mongelli turned his head in towards the blacks, noticing that two of them were in a heated discussion. One of them broke off the conversation and walked across the gym floor towards JP, who had his back to the black boy approaching him.

Terri was in JP's arms facing him. Looking over JP's shoulder, she watched Louis Washington approach them.

"Don't look now, my man, but we got company," she whispered softly in JP's ear.

JP turned as Washington approached him. The mood in the gym changed as both sides of the room stopped what they were doing and watched the confrontation. Officer Mongelli started to walk towards them anticipating trouble, but was held back by Father Martin. "Hold off, Bill. Let it play out."

"Ok, Father, but the first sign of trouble and I'm goin' in and crack some heads."

JP greeted the approaching teenager. "Aren't you on the wrong side of the fuckin' room, nigger?"

Washington ignored the remark. "Just a five minute truce, JP. I need to talk."

"Talk fast. You're cuttin' into my dance time."

"I'm talkin' to you because as much as I despise you and those honkies, you're the only one that's even half sane. Day before yesterday my sister left her cousin's home in Harlem and got on the Lex. She hasn't been seen since."

"What the fuck do I look like, the FBI?"

"Listen, man. The cops won't do nothin' cause she ain't white. Somethin' happened to her on the way home."

"What the fuck you want me to do about it, man. She's probably shackin' up in some sleazebag room with one of your nigger friends blowin' pot and fuckin' her brains out."

As much as he wanted to bash JP's face in, Washington held his temper. "She's nowhere in Harlem, and I don't know the Bronx that well to know where to look. We checked that Catholic hospital over at 233rd Street. They told us to go to the cops. Didn't even attempt to help. My boys believe your guys had somethin' to do with her disappearance. They don't need much to start an all out war. If your guys had nothin' to do with it, then you know enough dudes in the Bronx to ask questions. Maybe somebody knows something. I'm askin', man. It'll go a long way."

"First, mothafucker. Don't threaten me. I just gotta nod and you and your boys are dead meat. Second, I ain't your daddy. She's your sister. You find her. We don't beat on chicks, even when they are black. Look somewhere else, Washington. Now get the fuck outta my face. I got some dancin' to do."

"JP, you just another white trash motherfucker, that don't deserve to live. We may have to do somethin' about that. If we find she was fucked with by you or your boys, you're all goin' down!" He turned and walked away.

A moment later Tony Chicarella was by JP's side. "Let's take those bastards on now."

"Go back to hittin' on that broad you were chasing Tony. We start somethin' here it will give that cop Mongelli and the rest of those stooges a reason to beat on us." He turned to Terri. "Find someone to dance with, darlin'. I'm goin' out for a smoke." He didn't wait for an answer but walked past the cop and priest without acknowledging them and left the gym. He walked to the corner, lit a Camel, and leaned against the building.

JP's heart was beating like a trip hammer. It wasn't the confrontation that caused it but the feeling in his gut that this was going to be big trouble. He remembered Washington's sister. A real looker. Always took heaps of verbal abuse from the guys whenever she was catching the Lex or coming off the station. A lot of abuse, especially from Chicarella. He couldn't remember where he was the other night, he or Danny.

He heard a sound off to his side and turned looking for trouble. He stopped and watched her light a cigarette. The glow from the match in the shadows played tricks on him. She appeared to be more exotic, more beautiful in the subdued light. The flame from the match was reflected in her eyes, giving them a strange glow. His first thought was she was the most beautiful person he had ever encountered.

"What's the matter, white bread, afraid of a little colored girl?"

"You scared the hell outta me. What the hell do you want sneaking up on me like that?"

"Louis is my cousin."

"That's a problem you have to deal with. Did he send you out here to talk me into helping him? I told him where to find his sister. He just got to look a little harder."

"He doesn't know I'm out here. If he did, there would be hell to pay. Louis said for a white person you were the best of a bad lot. He must be thinkin' of someone else. Honkies like you think every black chick is a whore and on crack. Well, not Cynthia, and fuck you, JP." She ground her cigarette out and turned to go.

He grabbed her by the elbow and spun her around. She was inches from his face. "You didn't tell me your name, girl."

"It isn't girl! It's Tanya. Now let go of me!"

He twisted her arm around her back and pulled her to him, his lips finding hers. She struggled to free herself, tasting the salt on his lips as he pressed forward. She suddenly stopped struggling and kissed him back forcing his lips apart and darting her tongue to his. He relaxed his grip, and as he did she kneed him between his legs.

He went down holding his groin. "Motherfucker! You tryin' to kill me?"

He heard and then saw the switchblade she produced from her jeans. She held it to his throat as he struggled to rise.

"Don't move, white bread. What happened? You forget my name already. The next time you touch me I'll cut your throat! How did it feel kissing a real girl instead of those pasty lookin' bitches suckin' around you?"

"Now that I can breathe again, will you put that pig sticker away and let me get up."

She smiled bitterly, closed the stiletto and allowed him to rise.

"Thanks for nothin'" she retorted as she turned to go.

He laughed at her retreating figure. "I almost couldn't hear you; your heart was beatin' so fast."

She turned. "My heart was beatin' so fast because it was a rush kickin' you in the balls."

"We have to do that again sometime without the kneeing and the knifing."

She started walking away again. "Fuck you, JP. I'd rather kiss my dog."

He turned serious. "I'll make a deal with you, Tanya. We know a lot of people who have big ears in the Bronx. If somethin' happened to her up here it's already on the street. You guys don't know the Bronx, nor will anyone talk to a nig—black person. Also if somethin' did happen to her, I could probably find out by tomorrow. But I gotta tell ya. Anything happen to her, it happened in Harlem or the South Bronx, not up here."

She faced him. "What's the deal?"

"If I find somethin' out, you gotta have dinner with me."

"When pigs fly. There will be nothin' left of me if I'm seen with you, and there definitely be nothing' left of you. You goin' to sell me a line of shit and try to get into my pants, white bread? You want to see if fuckin' a black girl will change your luck? You want to brag to your friends that you bedded down a nigger and the color didn't rub off? Besides I'm only seventeen years old, but then you think black girls start fuckin' when they come outta the womb."

He smiled. "All that bullshit, and you know what? You didn't say no."

"You got somethin' to tell me tomorrow and then we'll talk, honky. How you goin' to get to me to let me know? You goin' to walk right into the projects looking for me? Maybe knock on my cousin's door?"

"You don't live in this neighborhood, because I wouldn't forget that face, so you'll be staying at the projects tonight. It's too late to take the subway down to Harlem. You may run into some bad people in that neck of town."

"A better class of people than up here." The anger had left her eyes. He thought it was a good sign.

"Tomorrow it's supposed to hit ninety, hot and muggy. Why don't you grab a few friends and head for Orchard Beach. Maybe I'll run into you at the at the concession stand in the Promenade on the boardwalk. Our groups are at opposite ends of the beach. The concession stands are located about the middle. Maybe I'll run into you around one o'clock."

"We blacks on one end and you honkies at the other, a little subtle segregation, right, JP."

"Well, at least we're on a first name basis again. I don't make the rules, Tanya."

"No but you bastards sure live by them, no matter how fucked up they are." She turned and walked back into the gym.

From the direction of the gym the soft lyrics of "I'm Sorry" by the Platters could be heard.

Chapter 13

1957—The Bronx

Tanya's head was spinning. *That no good son of a bitch! Thinks he can play me like a yo-yo. I've got to be crazy even tryin' to talk to him. If Louis knew he'd kill me. Fuck that honky and the beach. The man thinks he's hot shit comin' on to me like that. Cocky bastard! Those white trash bastards have a great philosophy. If it's black and male, kill it. If it's black and female fuck it, then kill it. She shook her head. Why the hell is this bothering me so much? He did know how to kiss, though. What the hell am I thinking!*

She walked over to the group of young blacks joining them as they were getting ready to leave, noting that Louis and Claude were having a heated exchange.

* * *

Tanya Reinford, approaching her eighteenth birthday, was not only beautiful, but brilliant. Gifted with an IQ of 160, she was already a member of Mensa, the high IQ society. She had skipped several grades and was scheduled to start college in the fall. Tanya had been interviewed by various colleges and knew she could go to Vassar with a full scholarship.

She was the product of an African American father who also boasted a high IQ and an Engineering degree from NYU, and a Japanese-American mother. They met in Hawaii a few months after the attack on Pearl Harbor. Captain Joshua Reinford was stationed in the Islands as an aide to Admiral Nimitz and was instrumental in planning the Battle of the Coral Sea. He was the highest ranking black soldier on the island.

Tanya's mother, Yokura Shimi, was an up-and-coming model and film star when they met. They fell in love and were planning to be married when orders came down to incarcerate all Japanese regardless of citizenship status. She was beautiful, intelligent, and fiercely independent. She spoke out vehemently against the imprisonment of American nationals making several enemies, and ruffling feathers in the Armed Services. Captain Reinford went to his superior, Admiral Nimitz, to plead his case. Nimitz disagreed with the new policy but had little choice in the edict. However, he did call in some favors, and as a result Yokura was not incarcerated.

They married and settled in Honolulu planning for their future. A year later they celebrated the birth of twins, Tanya and Peter. Joshua and Yokura loved military life, and Joshua's decision to make a career out of the Navy was reason for celebration. Yokura could still continue pursuing her career, another reason for celebration. One month before the United States ended the war with a bang, Joshua and Yokura decided to visit downtown Honolulu for dinner.

After an excellent dinner and a few drinks, they headed to their home in Kaneohe Bay. He took Route 3 to the Kaneohe cutoff, and then took the secondary road that would take them home. The road was dark, and the bright lights of the oncoming car in his lane caused him to swerve.

His car rolled over three times before it came to a stop. During the roll, the driver side door opened and Captain Reinford's left side was jammed against the doorpost, his left foot outside the car. As the car rolled over the door slammed shut severing his left foot at the calf. Yokura suffered severe trauma and lacerations to her head.

By the time the captain was released from the hospital in San Francisco, the war was over. He was discharged from the service with a medical disability, drawing a small pension. Yokura recovered but sustained a jagged scar from her temple to her jawbone. She also talked with a slight lisp as a result of her injury. Although still a beautiful woman, her career in modeling and films was over. They moved back to the states settling in Harlem, New York. With the servicemen returning from the war, there were very few high paying-jobs for a crippled black man with an Engineering degree.

His sister, a Maintenance Supervisor in Rockefeller Center, obtained a job for him as a maintenance technician, and Yokura started work as a seamstress in downtown Manhattan. They had a small apartment in Harlem. With the two paychecks and the small disability check they managed. Their love never wavered and they were dedicated to one another.

Yokura recognized early that both her children were exceptional, and she cultivated their talents, pushing them to excel in every undertaking they attempted. Their father helped to educate them using the skills he acquired in college and in the Navy.

They were latchkey children and spent many hours on the street, but under the watchful eyes of their family and friends.

Both children loved Harlem and its dynamics. Harlem was a city within a city with its own culture. It boasted the Apollo Theater with its renowned "Amateur Night" where many black entertainers such as Ella Fitzgerald got their start. The neighborhood was vibrant and alive. For the twins it was the best of all worlds.

Two years later Yokura gave birth to her third child. The birth was difficult, and she died never seeing the face of her new daughter. Joshua was left with the burden of raising his three children. Knowing his wife's dedication to their children's well being, he focused obsessively on the quality of their upbringing. The result was two children on their way to a better life. He had succeeded. He now concentrated on his youngest daughter Alicia. If possible, she was the most beautiful of the children. He and the twins doted on her. Her learning abilities served notice that she was a force to be reckoned with and she would give the twins competition.

When Tanya was 10 years old she performed in a school play. What was significant about this particular play on this particular day was the audience. Sitting among the crowd, mostly adoring families and friends of families was Emma Trice, editor and owner of Negro Digest, a weekly magazine catering to the African—American. She was in the process of starting another Magazine that also catered to the African-American community. It was to be a modeled after Life magazine. She needed someone to represent her publication to young, more affluent blacks. She was looking for someone beautiful and intelligent who could be molded into a spokesperson for the magazine now and in the future.

She had heard about the twins from her friends in Harlem and felt the young girl was worth a glimpse. The moment she saw Tanya she knew she had her candidate. Her first thought was if her brother were as smart and beautiful as Tanya she had a goldmine.

After much tutoring, brother and sister became the poster children for the magazine, modeling clothing and pushing merchandise that would had all black youngsters mimicking the two prodigies. The money the two children brought home from one sitting was more than their father made in a month. Their dream of going to college became a reality. Their father made sure they continued their education and with the help of Ms. Trice adjusted their schedules so as not to interfere with their schooling.

Trust funds were created for the children. They now had more than enough money to move out of Harlem, but rather than move, Joshua bought a row house on 128th Street, renovated it and redecorated it. He chose to stay where they were until the children started college. They would move after the children graduated. At the present time they were living well, using part of the income Tanya and Peter brought into the house. They wanted for nothing and started enjoying their lives. The future never looked better.

Joshua was disappointed when his brother-in-law James told him he was trying to get an apartment in a new housing development in the North Bronx.

"I need to get my kid's outta here, Joshua. It's starting to get bad down here with the drugs, gangs, and all that shit. The Bronx is like the country. The schools are better, and it gives the kids a better chance."

"I'm glad for you. Our family is tied to this community, but it will be great visiting you guys. Just like goin' to the country."

Chapter 14

1957—The Bronx

As Tanya approached the group, she overheard Claude telling Louis how they should go after a couple of the honkies and beat the hell out of them, until one of those mothafuckin' dogs talk. He was positive the white boys had something to do with Cynthia's disappearance. He wanted to grab one or two Berettas or Shack Boys and beat the truth out of them.

Louis was poking Claude in the chest with his finger. "Goddamn you, nigger, listen to me. Tomorrow we're heading down to the hood. I'm meetin' with some of the Dragons. Goin' to ask them to help. Need to make sure she left Harlem ok. If she did, we go after the white boys for answers. We can't get any answers from the pigs here. One of us walk into the 47th, they just as soon arrest us. When I called they told me somethin' about waitin' forty-eight hours before reportin' her missin'. Those sons of a bitches don't want nothin' to do with us."

Claude was furious. "You know how I feel about the truce with the Dragons. Those spic bastards are takin' over our neighborhood. Just as soon take out a couple of them along with that white trash."

"We need their help, Claude. Don't you fuck with any of them. If we go to war with these honkies we goin' to need all the help we can get!"

The path her cousin and the Kings were on frightened Tanya. No matter what the outcome of the inquiry, war with the whites appeared inevitable. If anything happened to Cynthia, the confrontation would happen very fast regardless of who was responsible. The Kings were looking to mix it up with the whites. They were tired of being pushed around on the Avenue. They were warned by the Guinea mobsters to cool it and not start trouble on the Avenue, as it would fuck up their dope trade. Louis was well aware if anything happened to Cynthia the Kings would ignore the mobsters and seek retribution regardless of the consequences.

Tanya's thoughts went back to the conversation she had with JP. Maybe he will find out something. Maybe he's a part of it. He seemed so sure of himself. She had to go to the beach tomorrow. She had to find out if he knows anything. If he did, she would know he and his friends were responsible. She was troubled by her feelings. She wanted to find her cousin. God only knows what happened to her. But deep down a part of her was hoping that JP had nothing to do with her disappearance. For one of the few times in her short life, she was not in control of her emotions and didn't understand why. She wished she could talk to Peter, but he would think her crazy. Besides, he was away for the weekend at some seminar.

She noticed the Berettas were leaving the gym. She didn't see JP among them.

JP was standing outside the gym smoking, his thoughts on Tanya,.

"W-What the fuck you doing man. You, p-playin' w-with dynamite fuckin' w-with that darkie."

JP turned took out his lighter, and lit Del's cigarette. "I'm givin' Grazio my car. Let him take Terri and some of the gang to White Castle for some hamburgers. You and I are goin' to the Sons of Sicily club. It's ten o'clock. Sally G should be there countin' the day's receipts. Need to talk to him."

"Now?"

"Now."

JP saw Grazio and Contelmo comin' out of the gym with Tina and Gracie, two of the Beretta Debs. He walked over to Frankie and handed him the keys to the car.

After explaining to Frankie what he wanted, he let Terri know he wasn't accompanying her.

"Where are you going?"

"I have to take care of some business. I'll try and catch you at the White Castle. Ok?"

"I'll just have Frankie drive me home. Fuck you if you think I'm going to wait around for you!"

"Whatever."

Del told his girlfriend Annie to catch a ride with Grazio, and he would catch up with her later.

Ten minutes later JP and Del pulled in front of a storefront with blackened windows. Gold lettering was pressed onto the window spelling out *Sons of Sicily Social Club*. Two men were sitting in chairs in front of the doorway watching JP and Del exit the car. Both men were dressed in casual slacks and tee shirts. Neither man carried a weapon, at least none that JP could see.

"Well, well. If it ain't the Beretta's. This a social call, JP?" The man who addressed JP weighed about two hundred eighty pounds, his bulk hiding the chair supporting him. The other man, half his size, said nothing, concentrating on grooming his fingernails with the tip of a six inch stiletto.

"Need to see Sally G, Gino. He around?"

"Watcha want him for?"

"Just tell him we're out here and need to talk to him."

Gino looked to the other man and nodded. The smaller man entered the store and a few minutes later came out. He retook his seat, looked at the boys, and gave them thumbs up. JP and Del entered the store.

The air conditioning sent a shiver through them, after coming in from the heat and humidity of the streets. The club was laid out railroad car style similar to many tenement apartments, long and narrow. It was divided into three rooms. A smoky haze hung over three oval tables and the small well stacked bar in the front room. Four men sat around one of the tables' playing cards, chips and money scattered around the table. A jukebox was situated in one corner, a Sinatra tune playing softly. The men ignored the two boys as Gino led them to a closed door. He knocked once and opened the door allowing the boys to enter.

Sally G was standing behind a long table, a small stack of bills in front of him. Off to the side was a five-gallon bucket filled with coins. It was the numbers take for the day. At least three-thousand dollars, thought JP. In his peripheral vision he noticed the figure sitting in a chair backed up against the wall, a stream of smoke curling from the cigar in his mouth. He sat, not acknowledging the boys, his eyes hooded by the hat he was wearing. JP recognized him immediately, and from the frightened look on his face, JP also recognized Albert Anastasia. The man, known as the Lord High Executioner, was boss of one of the New York crime families. JP wondered what in hell the mob boss was doing in this rat hole talking to Sally G. It was common knowledge that Anastasia was under tremendous pressure, struggling to retain his position as Boss of Bosses. His friend and mentor Frank Costello had been shot several months earlier forcing Costello to retire from his position as Boss of one of the five New York crime families. In June, Anastasia's hit man Frank Scalisi was gunned down in front of an Arthur Avenue produce market not more than a mile where they were standing.

At first JP's inclination was to turn and leave, but he realized he was not getting out of the club without an explanation. He decided to forge ahead.

"Sally, I need a favor."

"I'm pretty busy, guys. Let me finish countin' and then I'll talk to ya. I got somethin' for you guys anyway." Sally was nervous. A thin sheen of perspiration appeared on his forehead and above his lip. JP knew it was the presence of Anastasia that had Sally talking all business to them.

"Take a break, Sally. Let the boy's talk," Anastasia interrupted in a soft voice. "I wanna hear what's so important."

JP figured that *now* it was too late to turn around and leave. Del deferred to JP, figuring it was his dime.

"A black chick went missing day before yesterday. She's a sister to one of the Egyptian Kings, from Edenwald projects. The niggers think we might have somethin' to do with her disappearance. They've already been sniping at the white guys. They stoned one of our cars passing through their neighborhood earlier tonight. They were itching to mix it up after the dance, but there were too many cops around."

Sally and Anastasia exchanged hard looks. JP realized instantly they knew something about the girl. Del looked at JP with that "We're fucked" look.

Anastasia had an edge to his voice. "Did you?"

"Did we what?" JP asked, a puzzled look on his face.

"Did you and your guys have somethin' to do with her pounding."

"Her pounding? You know what happened?"

"You didn't answer the question, punk, and I'm really starting to get mad!"

Sally was keeping his mouth shut, listening to the dialogue between the young gangbanger and the Lord High Executioner and Boss of Bosses of the Cosa Nostra. Del said nothing, wondering if they were going to walk out of there in one piece.

"Fuck no, Mr. Anastasia. I can't speak for the other gangs but the Berettas are cool on this one."

"Then why do you care what happens to a nigger girl from the projects? She's just another *melenzana.*"

"We were told by your people not to start trouble on the Avenue. You told us to lay off because the blacks bring in the money from the numbers and the dope. You didn't want undo attention that could be caused by a race war. They're goin' to come after us sooner or later, and there will be a war, regardless of your threats. I don't know how long we can keep the peace. If we find the girl and let them know what happened or where she is, it might prolong the truce. It will buy some time until we can figure out how to keep the peace for the long term."

"You're full of shit, asshole. That's not the reason. You'll keep the peace for as long as I tell you. You fuck with our income, and you're dead meat." The mobster's voice was rising, and JP knew he was dangerously close to an ass whipping at the very least.

JP gambled. "Ok, it's not true. The broads got a cousin who's the most dynamite lookin' lady I ever laid eyes on. She hates white guys. If I tell her what happened to her cousin and where she is, I might get closer to her and work my way into her pants. I'm really hot for this chick."

Anastasia stared at him for a moment and then broke out in uncontrolled laughter. "A piece of ass, and a black one at that! You guys got no scruples!" He turned to Sally. "You mentioned that one of your runners came across a beat-up black chick. Thought it might mean somethin' to us."

Sally turned to Anastasia. "Anthony, you know we have eyes all over the Bronx. Our pimps, pushers, and runners tell us what's happening on the streets, leaving it to us to determine if it's important. One of our number runners works at Fordham Hospital as a cleaner. The reason why he mentioned this one to me is that she was thrown out of a car in front of the emergency room, beaten and near death. He said they patched her up, but she was in intensive care in a coma. She's listed as a Jane Doe. She may be the nigger's sister."

"You boys don't know anything about this?" Anastasia whispered the question, a dangerous look on his face.

Del spoke up at the risk of being mocked or even ignored because of his speech impediment. "W-We can p-put a spin on this in our f-favor." Sally knew of his affliction but said nothing. Anastasia just looked at him. "Go on."

"JP can t-tell h-her that she w-was thrown out of the Lexington Avenue Express at S-Simpson Street. H-He can tell her eyewitnesses saw it. That it w-was black guys or maybe Spics that did it. Take the h-heat off. Might cool t-things down. Let the niggers chase their tails."

JP and the two hoods stared at him. Finally Anastasia spoke up. "Smart. I like it. Do it, JP."

"That's ok as long as she stays in a coma. What happens when she regains consciousness?"

Anthony Anastasia stared at JP. "Maybe she won't come out of the coma, JP. Not your worry. You just want to dip your wick anyway."

"Thanks for the info. If it's ok, we'll be leaving."

"Not so fast, JP." Sally stopped them as they were turning to go. "I got a job for you and your boys. There's a new electronics store opening up on Bronxwood Avenue and 221st Street. He refuses to pay protection. I want you guys to rob the store and trash it. Bring the goods to our fence on Tremont Avenue."

"When?"

"Sunday night. We'll make sure the cops are busy elsewhere."

"Same cut?"

"Normally we go 60-40, but since we're helping you with your love life it's 70-30."

JP stared at him. "No problem, Sally." The two boys turned and left the club.

JP and Del didn't converse until they were in the car. Del started the car but didn't put it into gear.

He turned to JP. "I don't know w-what the fuck is going on, JP. You goin' to l-let me in on the s-secret? Is this all about g-getting into some black chick's p-pants? If I understand w-what w-went on in there, that broad in the h-hospital is as good as dead. I thought I w-was being cool, p-planting the idea that black guy's did it. I just signed h-her death warrant. That crazy bastard Anastasia h-has to kill h-her before s-she comes out of the coma. H-He can't risk h-her saying the w-wrong thing! W-what the fuck did I do? W-What happened to h-her, JP? W-Who the fuck did it?"

"It's not your fault, Johnny. I didn't see that coming either. It was a great idea. If we can keep the blacks and Puerto Ricans fighting among themselves, it's to our advantage. I made a date to meet that chick, Tanya, at Orchard Beach tomorrow and give her any information I had on her cousin."

"W-Whats w-with you and that broad? I ask y-you again. I-Is t-this all about you getting' into s-some black broad's pants?"

"I'm not sure what it is' Johnny. I need to see her. If she meets us tomorrow' I'll tell her where her cousin is and blame it on the spics or the blacks. It will buy some time."

"You k-keep s-saying it will buy us t-time' JP. Why do w-we need to buy t-time?"

"I think I know who brutalized that girl, Del. If I'm right' all hell is going to break out on this Avenue when and if she comes out of that coma. There's going to be a race war if the Egyptian Kings find out. We've been only sniping at each other over the last year because of the mob running interference. That's goin' to end, and after the smoke clears, there will be no Beretta's. We are goin' to be in a world of shit, Johnny."

"W-Who do you think did it, JP?"

"Between you and me, I think it was Tony, and he probably sucked Danny in to help him."

"Oh, Jesus Christ, no! Are you sure?"

"You're speech is improving, Johnny. You didn't stutter once. Yeh, I'm pretty sure. I don't know how Washington is going to react when he finds out what happened to her. I don't think he's going to believe the story about being thrown out of the subway. But we could buy a few days. We need to get the guys together tomorrow night after the beach. Keep an eye on Tony and Danny. Watch their reaction when I bring up the beating. Bet ya' an egg cream they give themselves away".

"W-what if the chick doesn't show up tomorrow?"

"She'll show up. She believes we had something to do with her cousin's disappearance and is gambling I'll have something for her. Besides, how can she resist a stud like me?"

"JP, h-how the fuck you can joke about this is beyond me."

Chapter 15

1957—Orchard Beach, the Bronx

Orchard Beach is a 115-acre, 1.1-mile-long, horseshoe-, shaped engineering marvel created on the shore of Long Island Sound by Parks Commissioner Robert Moses during the 1930s. Dubbed "The Riviera of New York", it consisted of 17 sections of sandy beach, a hexagonal-block promenade, a central pavilion with food stores and specialty shops, two playgrounds, two picnic areas, a large parking lot, and 26 courts for basketball, volleyball, and handball.

Backing up to Pelham Bay Park in the Bronx and situated between Rodman's Neck, and Hunter Island on Long Island sound, construction crews added white sand from the Rockaways in Queens and Sandy Hook, New Jersey, to the beach at a rate of 4,000 cubic yards a day. A 50-foot-wide promenade was built parallel to the shore, and a massive 1,400-foot-long, 250-foot-wide mall led to the 90,000 square-foot bathhouse, which also offered a restaurant and other concessions.

The last stop of the Pelham Bay Line of the New York Subway System is Pelham Bay Park. Using inexpensive transfer coupons, beach-bound commuters exited the subway and boarded buses that ran every 15 minutes, depositing their cargo at the beach's huge promenade. Additional buses ran from several points in the city directly to Orchard Beach making several stops along the way picking up sun worshipers heading for the shore.

On any given weekend the beach crowd exceeds 25,000 people. For a brief period time they forget the noise and hustle of the city. Cool breezes off the ocean and waves breaking in the surf replace the sound of the subways rumbling into stations, buses giving off their noxious fumes, and the dreariness of city life.

On this particular Saturday in July, the crowds came early in anticipation of record high temperatures. They laid out their blankets staking their claims and pushed their rented umbrellas into the sand. Outer clothing is discarded for bathing suits. Coolers, shoes and other belongings were used as anchors, holding down the corners of the blankets.

Standing on the boardwalk looking towards the beach, JP and Del saw a sea of umbrellas and blankets. Although it was only ten o'clock in the morning, the beach was already crowded. They had walked from the parking lot past the buses unloading the sea of humanity and through the promenade entrance to the boardwalk. They were leaning on the railing separating the beach from the boardwalk having a smoke, the perspiration soaking through their tee shirts. When they reached their destination they would shed their jeans, tee shirts, and sneakers, stripping down to their jockey-style bathing suits. They both scanned the crowds around the promenade, not to determine if any of the gang members were there but to determine if JP's "date" might be lounging near any of the food concessions. Not seeing her, JP's eyes drifted northeast towards Section One, where blacks and hispanics tended to migrate.

As if sensing his friend's disappointment, Del nudged him. "L-Lets go, JP. You t-told her about one o'clock. W-We'll c-come back later."

The boys turned and began walking southeast towards Section 17, where the white gangs and their girls congregated. By the time they completed their half-mile walk they were soaked in perspiration. They spotted several of the Berettas and accompanying females, their blankets laid out against the south jetty wall that extended from the boardwalk several hundred feet to the water. They left the boardwalk and made their way to the blankets through the already hot sand. Lounging on one of the blankets, several of the gang were playing cards. Three of the Shack Boys were spread-eagled on the sand trying to get a burn.

Towards the water he spotted Little Tom and Mike Scarpetta throwing a Frisbee around. He spotted Terri and a few of the Beretta

Debs in the water up to their waists trying to cool off but avoid getting their hair wet.

After acknowledging everyone, JP and Del shed their clothes and made for the water to cool off.

Grazio looked up from his cards and called after them. "Fair warning. Don't get their hair wet under penalty of death. Screw with their hair and the only love you're goin' get is with yourself."

Further down the jetty, closer to the water were some of the Golden Guineas. Several of the Fordham Daggers and their women took up space against the boardwalk wall. Other groups were spread out throughout the section. They all shared this part of the beach, comfortable with each other's presence, as long as the rules pertaining to the girls were not broken. This wasn't easy considering the dozens of girls in their bikinis parading up and down the beach eyeballing the guys through their dark sunglasses. The peaceful co-habitation of the gangs could turn into a brawl quickly if it was perceived that a rival gang member was hitting upon someone's girl.

It wasn't much different on the opposite end of the beach in Section One. The Egyptian Kings took up most of the space where the boardwalk met the beginning of the north jetty wall. Ten blankets were laid out, butting each other, forming a giant rectangle, with umbrellas scattered about. A dozen boys were spread out on the blankets reading magazines, playing cards, or just talking. Several of the guys were tossing a football around in the surf. Smaller gangs of teenagers were located across the area. They stayed to themselves taking care not to annoy the Kings in any way. The Kings dominated the beach, their numbers and reputation dictating respect. Even those gangs that made the trip from Harlem and Brooklyn recognized the fact that they were guests in another gang's territory and had to act accordingly.

Chapter 16

1957—Orchard Beach, The Bronx

Claude Brown, sitting on one of the blankets sucking on a Schaefer beer, scanned the beach. He noticed several of the Sabres, a Harlem gang, lounging on a blanket not to far removed. Also represented on the beach were the notorious Mau-Mau's from Brooklyn, and the Puerto Rican Viceroys from the South Bronx.

Neither his mind nor his attention was focused on the gangs populating the beach. He couldn't take his eyes off Tanya. She was standing among several of the King Debs laughing and talking. The white bikini she wore left little to the imagination. The duskiness of her skin against the white bathing suit created an image that drew stares of admiration from any man who came into visual contact with her. Claude was fixated on her. Not only was she beautiful, which was enough to prevent most guys from hitting on her, but she was also brilliant. He carried on a love-hate relationship with her. He despised her beauty and intelligence; she made him feel inferior; yet he couldn't help himself. He swore to himself she would one day be his lover.

Tanya never hinted that she was interested in him, but he was hopelessly in love with her. The thought of anyone else touching her infuriated him. If anyone did show an interest in her, he was quick to dissuade the potential suitor. She and two of the other girls started walking towards the boardwalk. She turned towards the blankets.

"We're heading to the promenade. Anybody want anything?"

Eugene raised himself up from the blanket. "Wait up, girl. We'll take a walk with you." He turned and stared at Clarence who was lying on his stomach reading the latest version of *Hot Rod* magazine. "C'mon, nigger, Get off your ass. We're goin' with the girls."

"Fuck you, Eugene. It's too hot to walk all the way down there. You thirsty, take a beer from the cooler."

Dehlia, one of the girls, turned to Eugene. "Don't bother comin', boy. We can find our way without your help. We don't need no chaperone. Besides we might meet some good lookin' guys instead of hanging round here with you."

A flash of anger crossed Eugene's face as he started towards Dahlia. "Shut your mouth, girl, before I shut it for you."

Tanya stepped in to defuse the confrontation. "Thanks, Eugene, but we really don't want a chaperone. We can take care of ourselves. We're just goin' for a walk. We're getting' bored."

Eugene stopped and looked at Tanya. "Every guy between here and the food court will be trying to hit on you. You're my best friend's cousin. I don't want some wiseass getting nasty with you, especially the way you broadcasting your sex."

"I was tryin' to be nice about this, Eugene. But fuck you. We don't want you to come along, and if a good lookin' nigger hits on me, I just may take him up on his offer. Let's go, Dahlia, I need an ice cream!"

Clarence looked up from his magazine. "Fuck 'em. Let them go. But she sure is some piece of ass," he commented as he watched them walk away.

"Shut the fuck up, Clarence." Eugene slid his jeans on and checked to make sure he had his knife. He waited until the girls reached the boardwalk and commenced to follow them, keeping his distance. Claude got off the blanket. "Wait up, Eugene. I'm comin.'"

Tanya and Dahlia made their way down the boardwalk chatting, totally oblivious to the admiring stares they were getting from the male population. Tanya's mind was on JP. Would he be there? Would he have some information for her? If he did it would only prove to her that he had something to do with his cousin's disappearance. She was anxious to see him, but she didn't understand her feelings. She needed to hate him but she couldn't. She kept visualizing his easy going manner, his self-assurance, and though she wouldn't admit it to herself, his good looks.

The boardwalk was crowded, and it was easy for Eugene and Claude to take advantage staying back in the crowd and still keep an eye on the girls. Guys of all color were passing remarks and wolf-whistling at the girls, some of them stopping in their tracks to admire the two women. Like Tanya, Dahlia, her slim ebony body strategically covered in a light pink bikini, was something to look at. Her skin shone with perspiration, which only added to her beauty. She had wide, luminous eyes, and sharp features. Her hair was done up in braids, a hint of pink lipstick on her full lips. Tanya always teased her, telling her she must have been the model for the visage of Cleopatra that adorned ancient Egyptian coins. She embarrassed easily, especially when receiving complements.

Tanya saw him before he spotted her. He and Del were leaning against the boardwalk railing across from the food court holding a couple of beers. They had just returned from Section 17 on JP's insistence. She had to show up, he thought.

She could tell he was looking for her the way he was perusing the crowd. Her heart started beating rapidly, and a feeling of anxiety came over her. She was angry at herself for being relieved to see him—and not because of any news of her cousin.

She asked Dahlia to get on line for an ice cream while she went to the restroom. Her skin glistened with perspiration brought on by the heat of the day and her own nervousness. When she was sure Dahlia was lost in the crowd of humanity surrounding the food kiosks, she turned and made her way to JP. She heard nothing except the waves breaking on the shore. It was as if someone turned the volume down on the inane chatter around her. As she made her way towards him, he turned and saw her. He smiled as she approached him.

"You're the most beautiful woman on this beach, Tanya," he said softly. Although he looked composed his heart was racing. His only thought was to grab her and kiss her, to feel her incredible body against his, to hold her tight. She saw he was perspiring freely, the droplets of perspiration running down his chest. She realized that no matter how cool he tried to appear, he was as nervous as she was, and she felt a little better. She wanted to brush her hand across his upper lip, wipe away the perspiration, and place her lips on his, remembering his last kiss.

Del watched the dynamics between the two of them and shook his head slowly, bringing the beer to his lips. Nothing but trouble, he thought. We are in for a world of shit.

"Do you have anything, JP?"

"I'm afraid I do, Tanya."

Del was watching the crowd in case of trouble. A white guy and a black chick spelled disaster, no matter how innocent the meeting. He nervously looked down the beach hoping to see some of the guys but spotted no one he knew. Several black guys came out of the restroom, saw the two talking, and stared angrily at them. Tanya and JP were going at it. Her back was to the crowd, and she was oblivious to the blacks spewing slurs at them. She was raising her voice, clenching and unclenching her fists, her body language displaying the anger and fear that was written on her face.

"You son-of-a-bitch," she screamed. "You and those white trash bastards from the Avenue did that to her. What kind of monsters are you?"

JP tried to calm her. "It wasn't our guys, Tanya. She was beaten and molested on the Lex. They threw her off the train at Simpson Street. A couple of bums on the platform saw it. The guys who did it were dark skinned, maybe spics or blacks. The bums went for the cops. It wasn't our guys," he pleaded. She started punching him in the chest over and over, crying. He grabbed her wrists to stop her, and calm her down. He noticed the two black guys pushing through the gathering crowd. "JP, w-watch your left," Del said softly. JP turned towards the threat, still holding on to Tanya's wrists, and saw Montgomery coming at him, pushing people aside.

"Fucker's got a p-pig sticker, JP."

"Yeah, and us in fuckin' bathing suits," he replied, letting go of Tanya. She looked confused and angry, tears streaming down her face. She turned her head towards the gathering crowd and saw Eugene and Claude closing in. Eugene was not bothering to hide the stiletto. As the crowd came into focus, she saw three other black boys throwing people aside, making their way to JP and Johnny.

Oh my God! What have I done! What have I done! This is my fault. They think he was hitting on me, she thought, as she watched the approaching assailants.

There was more commotion as the gathering crowd started to part. Two policemen pushed their way through the crowd, moving them back with their nightsticks. One of the cops spotted Montgomery holding the knife and went after him with his nightstick, dealing him a crushing blow to his head. As he fell to the floor the cop hit him again, targeting the arm holding the knife. Montgomery screamed and dropped the knife, his arm broken. The other officer unholstered his gun, stopping Claude. The other blacks backed off. Two police cars pulled up, and four more police exited the cars and waded into the crowd. The police were concentrating on the blacks, assuming they started the riot, rounding them up into a group, pushing them towards the police cars. The blacks knew enough not to offer any resistance, knowing they would be released, with the exception of Montgomery, who was dragged into one of the squad cars. Tanya and Dahlia were told by the officers to move on or they would be arrested. Tanya looked for JP, but he nor Del were anywhere to be seen. They simply walked away while the police were busy with the black youths.

Chapter 17

1957—The Bronx

He was furious, wanting to reach out and throttle her. She sat across from him sobbing uncontrollably.

"What the fuck were you doin', talkin' to that white trash bastard? You started a fuckin' riot and almost had Eugene killed."

"I didn't mean to start trouble, Louis. When he told me about Cynthia, I went crazy. I blamed him, and I lashed out. He was only telling me what he found out, after I asked him."

Louis sat next to her in the back of the car. Claude drove, Eugene riding shotgun, his right arm in a cast, caused by the mauling he received from the police. He was released after the authorities realized they had nothing to hold him on, and not wanting to explain his broken wrist, set him loose.

Eugene turned and faced them. "I'm tellin' you, Louis, she was all chummy with that honky motherfucker. Why in the fuck would he tell her where Cynthia is if he had nothin' to do with it?"

Tanya was shaken and distraught. "I met him outside the church when I went to have a cigarette. I called him a useless piece of shit, and told him he had no clout at all. He was a phony. He was trying to act like a big shot. He told me if I came to the beach today, he would find out what happened to Cynthia. I thought he was just showing off. When I saw him at the beach, and he told me what happened to her, I lost control and went at him. He didn't start it, I did. Eugene went crazy, thinking he was getting physical, and came at him with the knife."

"He told you she was dumped from the Lex at the Simpson Street Station by some guys who might have been black or spic, and you believe that?"

"Louis, that's why I went at him, I thought he was responsible. He kept denying it, saying it was a brother, or some of the Dragons that beat her."

Louis stared into her eyes. "Why was he so chummy with you with information, and wouldn't talk to me. You hot for that fucker Tanya? Is he hot for you? You forgetting you a black chick, Tanya? You forgettin' he's a white-trash gangbanger? Let me warn you, cousin, I ain't as dumb as I look. I find out there's something going on, I'll make sure you lose those pretty looks. You tell me he got the info on where she is from the Mafia boys. Why did they give him that info? Why did he go lookin' for it? What did you offer him in return, cousin?"

"Please, Louis; I don't know why he did it. Be thankful we found her. Dear God, please let her live."

Chapter 18

1977—Manhattan

Mike Scarpetta boarded the Amtrack in Fairfield, Connecticut, for the forty minute ride to Grand Central Station in Manhattan. He would then connect with the Lexington Avenue Express for the short ride to Wall Street, and his job as a Stock Broker with Schwab. Comfortably seated in the smoking car, he lit up a Camel and settled back to read the newspaper. His eyes immediately focused on the article relating to the murder of the priest. A sense of sadness and then anger came over him. Why would anyone harm Father Martin? How many times had the priest rescued the boys from the clutches of the police, always going to bat for them? A sad smile played on his face. The priest fought a losing battle, he thought. Most of the boys went into the rackets, becoming runners and gophers for the Anastasia gang. A few of them became made men in the mob, and sadly too many of them ended up in Rikers Island and Sing Sing Prison.

After the summer of '57 he followed JP and Del into the service. He could never forgive himself for what he had been part of that summer, twenty years ago. It was a recurring nightmare. He tried to distance himself from the horror by joining the Air Force, continuing his education, and joining the ranks of those few who escaped the Avenue.

His thoughts went back to the nightmare they unleashed and the fallout following that fateful night in 1957. The police were rounding up anyone who had an affiliation with the gangs, roughing them up, and trying to find someone to blame. Black detectives and patrolmen were transferred from Manhattan to the 47th Precinct to try to quell the anger in the black community, while organizations such as the NAACP and men like Martin Luther King tried to calm the gathering storm. The white gangs could put up with the police beating on them and the anger of the black community. What they truly feared most of all was retribution from the Cosa Nostra. With the crackdown on the gangbangers came a crackdown on the drug dealers. They couldn't push their drugs without fear of being caught. Every known pusher was being pulled in for questioning. Nothing was moving on the street. The gangbangers knew Anastasia was furious. The mob was losing thousands of dollars every day. It was Anastasia's responsibility to keep peace in the Bronx, and not bring undo heat on the mob. After that night, he had to answer to the five crime families.

Mike was jolted back to the present, noting that they were pulling into Grand Central Station. He made his way through the maze of humanity to the lower level where he waited for the Lex to pull into the station and carry him down to Wall Street. The platform was crowded with commuters waiting for the train to appear out of the darkness of the tunnel. The screeching of metal-on-metal signaled the arrival of the train as it took the long curve that brought it into the station. It was a sound that seared his mind and shook him to the core. The commuters pushed forward in anticipation of boarding the train as it rumbled to a stop, its hydraulic brakes forcing the seven-car, 270-ton-behemoth to slow down. As the train came to a halt, Mike pushed forward with the crowds entering through the now open doors. Suddenly, an agonizing pain surged through his body, forcing him to turn. He was now face-to-face with his assailant, and a look of surprise crossed his face as he recognized the person responsible for his pain.

"Say hello to Little Tom," his assailant whispered. The crowd continued to push forward, oblivious to the fatally wounded man. The momentum dragged him into the train. As the doors closed, he slid to the floor; the pain ebbing, being replaced by a blessed blackness.

Chapter 19

1977—Manhattan

He was totally oblivious to the breathtaking view the from his desk. His Manhattan office was located on the 77th floor of the north tower. The floor to-ceiling glass window gave a panoramic view of the southern tip of the Island and the Statue of Liberty, as well as a magnificent view of the Hudson River and the New Jersey Palisades. Although Starchip Headquarters was located in Seattle, the amount of time spent by the upper echelon on the East Coast warranted offices in Manhattan.

He couldn't take his eyes off the cover of *Business Week*. He had his feet propped up on the desk, the magazine resting in his lap. Tanya Reinford's beauty radiated from the cover. His eyes were riveted to the magazine cover. Although he had been following her career the last few years, he had never attempted to get in touch with her. He wondered if she ever thought of him without cursing. The last time he saw her, she was beaten and hurt, and placed the blame fully on him. She never wanted to see him or talk to him again. She just walked out of his life. Even now, he felt shudders of remorse course through him for losing her forever.

He read of her marriage with a sense of finality. She divorced eighteen months later, and even then he felt sadness for her. Back in 1957, after losing touch with her for several months, she showed up modeling for one of the big designer houses in Europe, and soon after, became a superstar and a shrewd business woman. He wondered what turned her life around. After Tanya he never found anyone to love for life, and settled on affairs and one night stands. Who was he kidding?

Tanya was a great short term affair. His loyalties lay with the whites. During his climb towards the inner circles of power and prestige, he could never go with, or marry a black. He would have been shunned and humiliated by the white community. He would have never gotten to where he was today with a black wife. It's much better now, and having her as a collaborator, with her intelligence and connections, would be a definite advantage. If anyone could revive those old feelings they had, he could.

He was tagged by the tabloids, and *People Magazine* as one of the most eligible bachelors in the country. Not only was he good looking, in a rough sort of way, he was also climbing in the ranks of the Fortune 500.

However, something is missing from my life, he mused. The something that's missing is staring at me from the cover of *Business Week*. As he stood captivated with her beauty, he began to believe they could grow beyond their past; that she would forgive him, and together they would pick up the pieces and repair their relationship. He rose from his desk, turned and stared out the window. Looking at his reflection in the glass, he shook his head. What a pathetic asshole you are, JP. What a pathetic *asshole.*

There was a short knock on his office door before it opened and Del entered.

"What's up, Partner? You're holdin' on to that magazine pretty tight. From the whipped look on your face, you must have Ms. Reinford on your mind."

Del was the CFO of Starchip. He was feared and respected by the competition. His recommendations and decision making were major factors in the success of Starchip. Him and JP complimented each other and were closer than brothers. Del was married to his childhood sweetheart from the Avenue. Their twin boys were in their teens. He owned a house in Seattle and a condo in Westchester, New York.

While serving in the Army he had lost his stutter through speech therapy. During their tour of duty, they attended classes dealing with computer theory, a fledgling subject at the time. After the service, the two of them attended college under the GI Bill. To raise money they worked part time for Sally G, running numbers and loan sharking for the mob. After college, JP was hired by IBM. Del's love for the financial sector drove him to get a doctorate in Finance. The gangs they knew in their younger days were gone. The Berettas, Guineas, and Daggers were relegated to oblivion. In the aftermath of the summer of 1957, many of the gangbangers left the Avenue, separating themselves from the street and one another. Although they kept in touch, they stopped socializing with each other and elected to find new friends, distancing themselves from the street life.

After five years with IBM, JP quit and formed a partnership with two other ex-IBM people, and they formulated the code that would eventually become the forerunner of the Internet. They picked up a contract with the Army to develop the code as a means of communicating within the Armed Services. Del bought into their enterprise handling all the administrative and financial duties. The rest was history.

"I'm in the mood for spaghetti with clam sauce. What do you say we get out of here, JP?"

"Yeah, I could use a drink anyway."

Although both men enjoyed good food and drink, they were in excellent physical shape. Both ran four miles a day, conditions permitting. They were always exercising in the company gym in Seattle and were members of a health club in New York. They were a haberdasher's dream with their proclivity for thousand dollar suits and the expensive accessories to go along with the suits.

"Before we leave, JP, give her a call."

JP knew exactly who Del was talking about. "Are you crazy? Do I look like a masochist?"

"Put it to bed, JP. The two of you have to get closure on this thing. You have to talk it out. Twenty years is a little long to drag this out. The playing field is level now. You're rich, powerful, and intelligent. The only advantage she holds over you is her looks. You fall far behind in that category, but you can't have everything."

"You're nuts, Johnny. First of all, she hates my guts. Second, getting in touch with her is impossible. Can you imagine the people she has blocking for her?"

"You could start off by congratulating her on her great success."

Del walked over to the desk and pressed the intercom.

"Yes, Mr. Pascalli"

"Adele, this is Del. I need you to find a number for Tanya Reinford. It's probably blocked and unlisted. Please get her private number."

"Mr. Delgardo, I would never do anything illegal."

"Of course not, Lydia. Have you got it yet?"

"I'll be back in a moment"

"JP, stop looking like I just stabbed you.

The intercom buzzed. "Mr. Delgardo, I have your number."

"It's her private number, right."

"That is what you asked me to obtain."

"Dial it for us Adele, and even with all your faults, we love you."

"Please pick up, Mr. Delgardo, your party is on the line."

"Well JP, Are you going to answer it?"

JP picked up the phone. "Tanya, this is JP."

Chapter 20

1957—The Bronx

Fordham Hospital, situated on Southern Boulevard near 189th Street, loomed grey and depressing. A huge four—story building surrounded by iron picket fencing, it gave the appearance of a prison rather than a hospital. Built in 1909 and located centrally, the hospital served people from all walks of life. On any given night, the emergency room was mobbed with the misery of life in the form of gunshot wounds, beatings, robbery victims, and accident sufferers. The hospital staff wore a look of defeat and weariness as they mechanically went about trying to stem the tide of humanity that continually passed through its portals. There seemed to no end to the pain and suffering.

Louis, Tanya, Eugene and Claude made their way into the emergency room through the doors directing them to the front desk. Stopping in front of the seated administrator, Louis waited until he was acknowledged.

"What can I do for you, young man?"

"I'm lookin' for my sister. She was brought in hurt. Her name is Cynthia Washington."

"When was she brought in here?"

"I believe she was brought in two days ago. She was beaten. I need to see her."

The administrator stared hard at him and looked through the admittance sheets for the past few days.

"There's no one registered by that name. Please hold on one moment." She looked in the direction of the entrance where two uniformed policemen were standing guard. One of the officers caught her look, and walked over to the small group.

"What's going on, Julia?" he asked the woman.

"This boy is looking for his sister. I believe it may be that Jane Doe that was brought in the other day. Can you bring him up to the ICU to see if he can make identification?"

"Come with me, son. You others wait here."

Louis, trailing the officer, said nothing on the way up to the 3rd floor, where the ICU was located. He felt as though his heart would burst. A feeling of helplessness and anger enveloped him as they stepped off the elevator. He felt as if the antiseptic smell enveloping the corridors was going to make him gag. The officer approached the desk and talked to the nurse sitting behind the counter. She picked up the phone and paged the doctor on shift. A moment later, a tall African-American male in a white smock came over to him. The badge pinned to his breast had the name Dr. Jonas printed on it.

"Mr. Washington?"

"Where's my sister? Why is she here in intensive care? How badly is she hurt?"

"Now listen carefully, Mr. Washington. We don't know if it's your sister. We need you to identify her, and if it is Cynthia, we will sit down and discuss her condition. One second, please."

The doctor walked over to the desk and told the nurse to make a phone call if the girl turns out to be the young man's sister. He walked back to Louis and asked him to come with him through the doors of the ICU. All the beds were occupied with patients, and it seemed to Louis that most looked like aliens with all the tubes, IVs, and monitors surrounding them. Several of the beds were encased in oxygen tents. They made their way down the aisle and stopped at the last bed. Tears sprung into his eyes, and he started to shake uncontrollably. She had bruises all over her face; an oxygen tube was inserted in her nose. Her head was bandaged, and there was a patch over her left eye. An IV was attached to one arm, and several machines gave off strange sounds as they monitored her vital signs. Louis fell to his knees, sobbing uncontrollably

"Cynthia, please wake up, please" he kept repeating over and over. Dr. Jonas helped him to his feet and escorted him out of the room to a small waiting area, and sat him down. Neither said a word for a time.

Louis slowly regained his composure, controlling the rage that burned within him.

"We need your parents down here as soon as possible. If you want, I will call them now."

"No! I need to tell them. I will do it in my way. What is going to happen to her? Please tell me."

"Your sister is in a coma. She's suffering multiple contusions over various parts of her body. She has a broken arm caused by her fall to the ground when she was thrown out of a moving vehicle. Her left eye is traumatized badly. The staff ophthalmologist believes she will recover her sight in that eye, but we'll know more after she comes out of the coma. Your sister was raped. We cannot determine how long she will remain in a coma, or if she will ever come out of it. She also has a head trauma that caused brain swelling. The swelling seems to be ebbing after the surgeon relieved the pressure. Hopefully there is no permanent damage."

"Mr. Washington, are you able to sit down with the floor nurse and give her some information? Also I informed the nurse to get in touch with the police. They will want to talk with you."

"This isn't a matter for the fuckin' police, Doctor. I'll handle it myself. You should know better. The police don't give a rat's ass about a black chick found beaten and raped. The only justice is goin' to come from me."

Dr. Jonas called the officer over. "Can you escort Mr. Washington to Admin and have him fill out some paperwork. Don't let him leave until you get a home phone number, and his parents are notified."

Forty minutes later, Louis stormed out of the Hospital, his small entourage following him. No one spoke until they got in the car. Eugene was behind the wheel, Louis riding shotgun.

Louis turned his head and stared at Tanya. "You listen to me, bitch," he said softly. The anger emanated off him in waves. He kept clenching and unclenching his hands as he spoke. "I don't know what the fuck is going on between you and that motherfucker JP, but we gonna find out here and now. My sister is lying' up there in a coma, beaten and raped. She was thrown out of a car in front of the hospital like a sack of shit. She wasn't beaten on no fuckin' train, and no brother did this to her. Now you tell me again how the fuck JP gave you that information. Why you? You doin' that piece of shit? Tell me now what's goin' on, or so help me cousin, I will throw you outta this car the same way my sister was thrown out of their car. Before I do that, I will fuck up that pretty face of yours permanently." He turned in his seat and faced her, a six inch stiletto in his hand.

She started talking, tears streaming down her face. Claude and Eugene said nothing, anger boiling up inside them. She started with the church dance, her confrontation with him outside the church, and the deal he offered her, if she would go out with him. She said nothing of the kiss. All she wanted to do is find Cynthia. She thought she could goad him into obtaining some information from the streets, and it worked. ""Please believe me, Louis. I only wanted to help. Thank God we found her."

Eugene spoke up for the first time. "We need to off that fucker. Let me do it, Louis."

Louis spoke up. "I don't think JP beat on her. As much as I hate the bastard, it's not his style. But he knows who did beat on her, and if we go after him, he's not goin' to tell us shit, and the boys who did this are goin' to walk. No, I have a better idea. My little cousin is goin' to keep that date with JP and is goin' to find out who is responsible."

"You ain't goin' let her go out with him. Are you nuts?"

"Shut the fuck up, Eugene, and watch the road. We play it my way, and if it doesn't work, we take all those fuckin' Berettas down."

"Don't *I* have a say, Louis? You want me to be *bait* for you? I'm scared!" The tears were falling freely from Tanya's eyes.

"You'll do what the fuck' I say, girl. You get in touch with him, and you play him like a five-dollar whore if you have to, but you goin' get me some names!"

Chapter 21

1957—The Bronx

The sun was slowly setting in the west; the tall steel beams supporting the elevated tracks casting giant shadows; the gaps in the steel structure highlighting the dust motes kicked up by the vehicular traffic that passed under the steel rails. A hot breeze trapped by the stores on both sides of the street was blowing continually, making it seem even warmer then the ninety-degree temperature. The smell of oil from the constant flow of traffic and the elevated line above street permeated the air. JP, dressed in his traditional jeans and white tee shirt, walked into Aaron Slotnick's store.

Tony and Danny were sitting at the counter sucking on sodas and reading comic books borrowed from the magazine rack. No matter how many times Slotnick yelled at them to buy the merchandise or leave it alone, his pleas always fell on deaf ears. He would just shake his head and be thankful the little thugs didn't wreck his store. Besides, they did pay for what they bought. Danny looked nervous, JP thought. His eyes flitted all over as if he were going to be attacked from behind. Tony seemed oblivious to his surroundings and was engrossed in the latest problems concerning Archie, Veronica and Betty. Without looking up, Tony greeted JP. "How come Archie gets all the pussy? He's such a loser."

JP took a camel from the twenty to thirty loose cigarettes lying in the cigar box on the counter. Slotnick sold them for two cents each to anyone who didn't want to pay for a pack or couldn't afford the price. JP sat at the counter and asked Slotnick for a chocolate egg cream.

"Tell me something, Aaron. Why do they call them egg creams when they contain syrup, seltzer, and milk? Ain't no eggs or cream in them."

"So how would I know? You're the brainy one in this crowd. You tell me, and you owe me five cents for the egg cream, and two cents for the cigarette." JP tossed a quarter on the counter and turned to Tony and Danny

"Interested in making some extra money tonight? It would be a four-man job. You two, Del, and myself. It's for Sally G. Could be worth a couple hundred bucks."

"Sure, what time?" Tony queried.

"Meet down the pool room around ten. I'll fill you in, and then we go. I'm heading for the pool room now. See you later." JP got up, took his change and started to walk out. "By the way, Tony. How did you get those scratches on your face?"

"Angry broad. Didn't like my grabbin' her teat."

"Looks like you got the worst of it.

Tony laughed. "I don't think so."

Before JP could answer him, Aaron stopped him and led him around the counter. "Something for you. This is trouble, JP. The young negro girl, she gave it to me and then took the stairs to the downtown Lex."

He handed the folded note to JP and walked to the back of the store shaking his head. JP walked outside unfolding the piece of paper.

Please call me tonight. Here is my number. I'll be at home, not at the projects

JP read the note again and went back into the candy store. He walked to the rear where the two phone booths were located. He stepped in the booth, closed the door, and slid a dime into the coin slot. He dialed the number, his hand shaking slightly. *Now, what the hell is that,* he mused? As the connection was made he felt his heart beating a little faster. *This is fuckin' crazy,* he thought, as the phone was picked up at the distant end.

"This is Tanya. Who's calling?" came softly over the wire. Now he knew his heart was beating a little faster. "This is JP, Tanya."

"Can you meet me tonight, JP? I'm sorry about the beach, and I don't renege on my promises. Can we meet somewhere where we won't be seen? About nine o'clock, maybe in Manhattan somewhere?"

"There's a restaurant named Forlini's on Baxter Street, in Chinatown. If you take the Lex get off at Canal Street. Baxter is one street over. If you get there before me, reserve a table and wait for me."

"I'll see you at nine, JP."

JP hung up and stared at the phone. Washington is pushing her, he thought. He wants information, and he's using her to get it. This is goin' to get really interesting. He opened the door and exited the phone booth. Danny and Tony were still at the counter. They were joined by several other Berettas: Bobby Contelmo, Little Tom, and Del.

"Let's go down the pool room. We need to talk."

"What's up, JP."

"We'll talk downstairs."

The pool room was situated two doors down from Slotnicks and was located two stories underground. There were fourteen pool tables, two billiard tables and nine bowling alleys. Between the rooms that housed the pool tables and the bowling alleys, a small restaurant, bar, and a command center for the establishment were located. The noise level was high. The bowling balls hitting the pins and the clatter of pool balls from the ten or twelve pool tables being used, caused quite a commotion. Those sounds, coupled with the voices of twenty or thirty players and spectators, made it difficult to carry on a conversation

A cloudy haze of smoke hung over the tables caused by the chalk dust, cigarette, and cigar smoke. The room had a musty smell. Every table was illuminated by two large circular lights that dropped down from the ceiling. The lights over tables not being used were turned off. The atmosphere gave the impression of continual twilight. The players ignored the din around them and concentrated within their own universe. Money continually changed hands as games of straight pool, Chicago, pill pool, nine ball and eight ball ended, and new games commenced.

They walked down the two flights of stairs and entered the pool room. Angie Spedino and Benny Coletta, two of the Shack Boys, were at the small bar having a beer. The owner, Gus Letto, knew some of the boys were underage; but as long as they had an ID, phony or legitimate, he served them. His payoffs to the inspectors and the police took care of any violations that existed.

Del asked Gus to turn the lights on over table twelve, one of the billiards tables. These tables were larger and contained no pockets It was located in the right rear of the pool room, away from the normal size pool tables. JP motioned to Angie to join them. They all made their way back to the table, now illuminated, and gathered.

"First, Sally G has some work for us tonight," JP started. Del, Tony, and Danny have volunteered. I was to be the fourth, however; something came up and I can't make it. Angie, are any of your boys interested in filling in for me?"

"I'll do it," Benny ventured. "I could use some spending money."

"Good! Stick around after we break, and I'll fill the four of you in on the job."

JP paused, and then rubbed his eyes. "We have a potential major problem that can impact all of us on the Avenue, as well as the other gangs and it's serious."

Del knew what was coming and kept an eye on Tony and Danny, for their reaction.

"Two days ago, the sister of one of the Egyptian Kings went missing. That's why Louis Washington braced me at the church. He asked me to help find her. He wanted to call a truce. I told him to fuck off. Well, she's been found. She's in Fordham Hospital, in a coma. Apparently she was beaten badly."

Del caught the glances between Danny and Tony. *We're fucked*, he thought, *they're responsible*.

Angie spoke up. "What's that got to do with us, JP? We don't fuck with any chicks. It's the code! It has to be some nigger or maybe some spic nailed her down in the Fordham area. What's with that showdown you had at the beach yesterday? Did those niggers come after you because they think we had something to do with the beating?"

Tony jumped in. "They came after him because he was hittin' on one of the darkies. They don't like the idea. Right, JP?"

"Tony, you're an asshole and nothin' going change that; except one of these days I'm going to pound your ass into the ground. You got somethin' more to say, say it"

"I was only fuckin' around, JP. Back off."

JP continued. "In regards to your question, the Egyptian Kings are in a wait mode. If it was up to Eugene Montgomery, they would use the chick's beating as an excuse to start an all-out war. Washington is holding them back, waiting to see if she comes out of the coma. I got this from Sally G. He said if she comes out of the coma and names a white person or persons, that person will be handed over to the Kings regardless of which gang they belong to;, and it's not an option. If he or they are not handed over, Anastasia and the mob will come down on us big time."

Angie banged his fist on the table. "No white boy will be handed over. We do that and we're ruined on the Avenue. Same goes for the Daggers and the Guineas. They won't hand over one of their boys to the niggers!"

"I know that, Angie. It means we will not only be at odds with the blacks, but also the mob. They want nothing interfering with the trade. An all out race war would cause chaos here in the North Bronx."

Del was watching Danny light a cigarette. He was sweating profusely and his hand shook when he lit the smoke.

"You feel ok, Danny?"

"Yeh, I'm fine, Del.

Tony spoke. "It's a moot point. She ain't comin' out of that coma. Someone will see to that. Sally G knows none of the gangs would hand over one of their own to the blacks to be offed. You think the mob isn't contemplating doin' her. It would be the easiest solution."

JP looked directly into Tony's eyes. "You better hope, Tony; you better hope. I'll keep you guys up to date. Can I get with you guys goin' on the job tonight?"

Chapter 22

1957—West Harlem, Manhattan

Louis Washington looked across the table at Jose Lopez, leader of the Dragons, a Spanish-American gang residing in West Harlem. The Harlem contingent of the Egyptian Kings and the Dragons were going through an uneasy truce; there was no love lost between the two gangs. Louis had called this meeting with Lopez and Quincy Adams, leader of the Egyptian Kings in Harlem.

They were sitting in a small store that served as a clubhouse for the Dragons. The windows were blacked out, and the smoke-filled room did little to brighten up the dim lighting. Several of the Dragons were sitting around on a couple of beat-up, ripped sofas; smoking joints, and guzzling beer. The table the three gang leaders were sitting around was located in the middle of the room. Lopez opened a few bottles of beer taken from a beat-up ice box that was sitting in one of the corners. The room smelled of habaneras, guajillo chiles, beans, roasted pork, and marijuana. "It's you're nickel, Washington. What do you want from us?"

Washington told them of the beating his sister endured, the attempt to place blame on the Dragons, or the brothers, and his suspicion as to who the perpetrators were that brutalized and raped his sister.

Adams banged his fist on the table. "Why the fuck don't you just go after the fuckers now and put them under?"

Washington looked him in the eyes. "I plan on offin' anybody involved. The Bronx, and by default, the Avenue is controlled by one of the Five families. I'm not tellin' you anythin' you don't know.

Anastasia runs the Bronx family. They control the drugs, numbers, loan sharking, and protection rackets. They don't want anything to happen. Those fuckin' wops run everythin'. If we go after them now as a gang it will bring the cops down on us big time. They'll shut everything down. The result will be that crazy bastard Anastasia coming after us with a vengeance."

"Then what the fuck you gonna do, bro?" Lopez countered.

"My sister could come outta her coma soon, the Doctor says. When she does, she'll name the bastards who done her. If they're white boys from one of the gangs, I tell that gang to hand them over to the Kings. We'll put them in the ground."

"What in the fuck makes you think they'll hand over one of their own? They would look like wimps and pussies. The other gangs would turn on them in a heartbeat. Ain't goin' to happen bro."

"I know that. I'm countin' on it, in fact. They don't turn them over, we gotta reason to go after them. I think the mob will go after the white boys for hurtin' their bottom line."

"Why you talkin' to us?" Lopez asked.

"I have a gut feelin' the boys I want are members of the Berettas. Don't ask me why? If we come down the Avenue with force, the Berettas will turn to the other white gangs for help. They gotta help them. We niggers raidin' them on their turf is somethin' that would bring them together faster than an opportunity to gangbang a movie star. We would be outnumbered and on their turf. We wouldn't stand a chance."

"So you want us to help you, if you decide on an all-out war."

"Think about it. We pick the time. Your boys and yours," pointing at Adams; "together with the Viceroys and the Enchanters, could number sixty or seventy guys. At an agreed upon time, bring your boys up from Harlem. We don't need a lot of cars. The Lex stops right at their door. We beat their asses, and we take over the Avenue for good. White Plains Road will be ours from Fordham Road to 241st Street. Let whitey be afraid to walk the streets for a change."

"Seems like a lot of ifs." Adams countered.

"Whatta us spics get outta this? Why do we care?" Lopez challenged

"You care because more and more of your people are moving up there. You see that! You're gonna want a foothold up there and equal footing with the Kings." Between our people and yours we can own the Avenue!"

"The mob might have somethin' to say 'bout that, bro'."

"The mob don't care about nothin' but makin' money. They become awful colorblind when it impacts their pocket. I want the fuckers who put my sister in the hospital. The white boys gonna have a little trouble protectin' one of their own during a war."

Lopez leaned forward. "What if your sister doesn't make it, man? Then you got nothin'. What you gonna do then?"

"I can't think that way. She's gotta make it."

Chapter 23

1957—The Bronx

It was raining softly but steadily, the warm air making the Avenue feel akin to a giant sauna. Dusk was beginning to push the daylight away, making way for the night. Typically Sundays were quiet; a family day to be spent with loved ones, sitting down to dinner or attending houses of worship. For most, it was a day of rest in preparation for another week of drudgery at work.

The four young gangbangers were standing under the metal stairs that led to the station platform above, keeping dry. They were waiting for the darkness, preparing for the job ahead. Tony and Del would climb to the roof using the fire escape at the rear of the store. They would jimmy the skylight open and Tony would shimmy down the knotted rope they brought with them into the store's interior. Several burlap bags would be dropped through the skylight. Tony would fill them, and Del would hoist them up to the roof. Tony would then trash the store and shimmy up the rope. Benny would park his '51 caddy on the corner of 220th Street and Bronxwood Avenue, Danny, in his Chevy coupe on the corner of 221st and Bronxwood Avenue. The store was located mid block. Both cars could be seen from the roof. Del would keep his eye on the vehicles. If something went wrong they would flash their headlights, the signal to abort and get out. According to Sally G, the police car that patrolled that neighborhood would be parked at the Baychester Diner, several blocks from the store; the occupants having their free hamburger and fries. It was also noted that the store had not installed a working alarm system. It was to be installed in the coming week.

All this information was obtained from police informants assigned to the 47th Precinct, who were also on the mob's payroll. After the robbery, Del would call Sally G at the club to give him status. They would then drop the goods off at the fence. The job was a piece of cake.

* * *

It was going on 8 pm. JP headed downtown to meet Tanya at Forlini's. He had dressed carefully before leaving the house. He wore a white short sleeved pullover tucked into his black slacks with white saddle stitching. The pants were tapered at the bottom to fourteen inches. They fell neatly over the highly glossed pointed dress shoes, affectionately known as "cockroach killers". The rise from the belt loops to the waist was two inches. He carefully combed his hair into the preferred duck's-ass-cut favored by the gangbangers. The small amount of Brylcreem allowed his hair to stay in place and gave it a shine.

His cousin Lou loaned him his '55 Ford Fairlane convertible for the evening in lieu of his own banged up Fairlane. It went with a warning that if he so much as found a scratch on it, he would personally cut off JP's balls.

Tanya was sitting on the steps in front of her apartment waiting for her friend Dorothy. She had told her father that Dorothy and her were going to the Apollo Theater on 125th Street to see rock and roll star Dale Hawkins, one of the first white people to perform on that stage. His hit record "Susie Q" was topping the charts that summer. In actuality, she did have tickets for the show, but she talked her brother Peter into taking her friend Dorothy. The fact that Dorothy had a mad crush on Peter helped tremendously. To Peter it was a great relief not to be going with his sister. Taking Dorothy was a coup, a feather in his cap. Tall, slim with patrician features, she carried herself with confidence. She was fun to be with and a gifted conversationalist. She and Peter made a good looking couple who enjoyed each other's companionship. He was looking forward to the coming date.

Peter questioned Tanya incessantly about her change in plans. She refused to reveal them to him, only to say that she had an important date.

"The way you're dressed it must be important. Who is he, Tanya? I'm your brother and I'm uncomfortable fooling Dad like this? It's not like you."

"Just trust me, Peter. I promise you I am doing nothing wrong. I will tell you everything tomorrow. By the way, you better watch yourself with Dorothy tonight. Remember she's my best friend, and she will tell me everything when I see her."

She thought about his comment on her dress. Did she overdo it? The pale yellow skirt and the white short sleeved scooped-neck blouse brought out the beauty of her light brown skin. Her accessories were limited to looped earrings and an unobtrusive small gold cross joined to a slim gold necklace. Her long hair was combed into a French twist making her appear older; as did the stiletto heels she wore.

Peter rose as he saw Dorothy coming out of the apartment complex next door. "Be careful little sister. I'll see you later." He bent over and kissed Tanya on the cheek.

"Hey, you are my date, buster." Dorothy smiled as she walked over and kissed Peter. "We're atta' here, Tanya. I don't know what's going on but I'm worried about you."

"Stop worrying and have a good time." Tanya stood and hugged her friend. She watched them walk down the street just as the gypsy cab pulled up to the curb. They were called gypsy cabs because they did not carry a taxicab license issued by the city. These companies' were not allowed to pick up customers on the street but their drivers often roamed the city hoping for an illegal pickup. The customer called into a central office with a pick-up address that in turn was relayed to a cruising cab. This particular company worked out of a storefront on 128th Street and Third Avenue.

"Forlini's, right, sister? Nice place. Never could figure an Italian restaurant in the middle of Chinatown."

Chapter 24

1957—The Bronx

The job went off without a hitch. All the cases in the store were cleaned out. The stolen goods were placed into the burlap bags, and hoisted up through the skylight to the roof by Del. He then signaled Danny with a small pencil light. Danny drove his car around the back of the store, and the goods were brought down the fire escape and into the trunk of Danny's car. As soon as they were secure, Danny took off. Del went back up to the roof and waited for Tony to finish trashing the store. They collected the rope and made their way down the fire escape where Benny was waiting for them.

They drove south on Bronxwood Avenue until they crossed Route One. Benny pulled into the White Castle on Allerton Avenue where Danny was waiting for them. Benny, Danny, and Tony went into the White Castle and ordered a couple of dozen of the miniature hamburgers while Del called Sally G from the pay phone. The boys came out of the White Castle and sat at one of the few empty tables eating the hamburgers while Del concluded the phone call.

Although it was a Sunday night, the establishment was jumping. It was crowded with young people. Club shirts were prevalent everywhere; gangs showing off their colors. The night belonged to them. They all had one common thread running through them. They were all white.

The proprietors gave up trying to chase them, weighing the loss of some family business against the money the gangbangers spent. There was very rarely trouble; at the very least, it was quickly contained. The three Berettas passed pleasantries with some of the other teenagers while waiting for Del to get off the phone. Tony had one of the Dagger Debs cornered, putting a pass on her, when in his peripheral vision he noticed Father Martin making his way through the knots of teenagers.

The priest walked over to Tony. "Hey, Tony got a minute?"

"Does it look like I got a minute? I'm pretty busy here, Father. You're breaking my concentration. Besides, isn't kind of late for you to be roaming around? You better buy a couple dozen burgers to take back to the church, or people are going to start talking."

"I'm looking for JP? Is he around anywhere?"

"What am I, his fuckin' brother?"

"When you see him tell him I need to talk to him regarding his conversation with Louis Washington." He started to walk away, but suddenly turned and grabbed Tony by his throat, shoving him against the wall. "You will respect me and what I represent. If you talk to me using that language again, I will knock you on your ass, you understand?" He turned and made his way into the restaurant stopping to talk to some of the teenagers. Tony was livid, clenching and unclenching his fists. The girl he was trying so hard to impress was laughing. "Maybe if you go to confession he'll be nicer to you, Tony." She walked away, back to her own group of people. He knew she was going to tell the group of Daggers what happened, but he knew better than to lash into her with all the Daggers lounging about.

He walked back to the table and sat down. "What the fuck is keeping Johnny? He's been on that phone forever."

Del exited the phone booth and sat at the table.

"Change of p-plans, boys. Sally G said our f-fence on Tremont Avenue can't service us. H-he thinks h-he's under surveillance. W-We have drop the stuff off at Q-Quan Lees'."

"All the way down to Chinatown? That's an hour's drive." Benny was pissed. "It's 11 o'clock Johnny."

"W-We don't all h-have to go. I'll drive. W-Who's going to keep me company?"

"I'll tag along. Always did like prowling downtown."

"Ok, Tony. Let's get going. Sally G is going to call Quan Lee and let him know w-we're on our w-way. W-we'll catch up w-with you guy's tomorrow. Sally G w-will let us know how much w-we're getting for the stuff."

Tony smiled. "Mott Street, here we come. Maybe we'll latch on to some Chinese pussy."

Chapter 25

1957—Manhattan

Forlini's was a family owned Italian eatery located underground on Baxter Street on the edge of Chinatown. Away from the touristy Mott Street and Mulberry Street, it catered to local patrons. Due to its proximity to the courthouses in lower Manhattan, it was a haven for politicians, lawyers, and Judges. Ironically it was also the hangout for many of the Italian hoodlums who controlled Little Italy and the Bowery.

The walls were decorated with oil paintings—depictions of the Old Country, with fat-old men playing the fiddle and getting drunk. The dining area was split into two rooms. Both were constantly occupied with patrons gorging themselves on the Italian fare being offered. Adjoining the front dining room, Forlini's boasted one of the few remaining bars in Chinatown, perfect for before-dinner drinks or as a rendezvous point.

JP looked at his watch for the fifth time in the last five minutes. It was almost 9:30. She was going to stand him up. He was pacing back and forth in front of the restaurant as customers entered and exited. Assuming she was traveling by train, he did not immediately check the gypsy cab that came to a stop. His heart skipped a beat as she exited the cab. She was the most beautiful woman on the planet, he thought. She walked towards him, a puzzled look on her face.

"You have a very stupid look on your face, JP."

He couldn't speak for a moment. He finally found his voice. "I thought you weren't coming. You're late."

"Should I leave?"

"No! I don't care if you're late. I'm just glad you're here. I wasn't sure you would find the place. I picked it purposely because it was a little out of the way."

"I've been here before, JP. Can we go in? I'm starving."

Actually she had butterflies in her stomach, and she was a nervous wreck. She didn't understand it. She should despise this person, but she was glad to see him.

They walked down the stairs and entered the restaurant. The maître d' escorted them to the rear room and sat them at a booth that gave them privacy. He walked away ten dollars richer for his trouble. A few minutes later a waiter appeared at their table.

Two glasses of Chianti, please." The waiter stared at them for a moment debating if he should ask for an ID. He decided against it.

"Very good, sir. Here are some menus. The specials are listed on a separate sheet."

She was staring at him, a small smile playing on her face. "How do you know I wanted a glass of wine? I am underage, you know."

"Should I call him back?"

"No, Chianti is fine."

"You said you were here before? With your father?"

"No, my agent."

"Right. You are somewhat of a celebrity. I suppose you're independently wealthy, and that really begs the question of why you are still living in Harlem."

"It's convenient, and my brother and I have many friends there. It's not all slums and decaying tenements."

"If I offended you, I'm sorry. You called this truce, and I would probably give you odds you're here because your cousin wants information as to who brutalized his sister."

The waiter appeared with their wine and asked if they were ready to order. Tanya suggested they start the meal with an appetizer of calamari fra-diavolo.

"An excellent choice, signorina. I shall place the order immediately."

"I'm surprised you like squid, and in a spicy sauce no less."

"Do you think we just eat chittlin' and ham hocks JP? By the way, you're right. I'm here because my cousin is convinced you had something to do with the beating. How did you know where she was, and you lied about her being assaulted on the Lex."

He stared into her eyes for a moment and then spoke.

"Truthfully, I don't know for sure who is responsible. I have my suspicions but no proof. She was taken to the hospital in a car and dropped in front of the emergency room. I was told this by one of the mob guys. They have eyes and ears all over the city. Very little gets past them. You're cousin Louis and his buddies are not the only people looking for the garbage that did this. The mob wants them, and we want them. This is ready to break out into a race war. Let me give you a couple of situations. I know you're a brilliant girl, and are light years ahead of us peasants in the brain department, and you're going to Vassar in the fall. But as smart as you are, you're not streetwise. You and I, and everyone surrounding us, are sitting on a time bomb with a very short fuse."

The waiter appeared with the appetizer, spooned some of the seafood into each dish. "Are you ready to order or do you need more time?"

"We're not ready, yet. Can you give us a little more time, and bring us another glass of wine?"

Tanya picked at her food. "Educate me, JP."

"If your cousin comes out of her coma and identifies the assholes that assaulted her, the Kings are going to want blood. They will go after the people responsible, wanting no interference. If these thugs are gang members, and they probably are, their gang is not going to allow that to happen. If it were one or more of our guys, we couldn't give them up to the Kings, for that would show us as weak, and it would reflect on all the gangs. The white boys would surround the wagons to protect their own. That would compel the Kings, and the other black gangs associated with them to force our hand and the result would be an all-out race war. Aside from the chaos and bloodbath an outbreak like this would cause, there is a much bigger concern. The rackets would take a big hit. Drug traffic would slow down to a crawl. There would be no income from the numbers or shylocking or betting on the horses. Not to mention the presence of a beefed up police force. The mob would come after us, and by us, I mean black and white. Trust me, they couldn't care less who they hurt, maim, or kill to restore the status quo. The boys who beat your cousin would disappear along with anyone who protects them. The Kings would be beaten into submission by the Mafia's strong arm boys. It would take the mob weeks or maybe months to recover their losses. Are you starting to get the picture, Tanya?"

She looked at him, horrified. "You said a couple of possibilities. What could be worse?" Tears came to her eyes as she answered her own question. "What could be worse is that she doesn't come out of the coma. That she dies! If she can't name her assailants, they could sit on the problem, believing it may go away." She sat back, tears streaming down her face.

"Tanya, Albert Anastasia is not called the Executioner for nothing. He has killed and had people killed, for a lot less. He's under the gun with the five families. Vito Genovese wants him replaced. If this problem doesn't go away, the loss of revenue to the mob will give the Families a reason to get rid of Anastasia. He has to do something! You need to explain this to Louis, and you need to call him now. Someone from his family should be at the hospital at all times. There is no sense going to the police; they won't help. He also has to be made to understand that this has to be worked out without an all-out war."

"JP, if it turned out it was someone in the Berettas who did this, would you give them up?"

"No."

"Then there is no answer. You're problem, JP, is that you want to be decent. You just don't know how.

"I'm going to the phone, JP." She rose from the table in search of a phone.

JP sipped his wine and checked out the room. Sitting at a large corner table, two men JP never met, but knew well, were sharing a large antipasto and a bottle of wine. Vito Genovese, head of one of the five families and Crazy Joey Gallo, a made man and vicious killer were in a heated exchange speaking in Italian. It was common knowledge on the street bad blood existed between Genovese and Anastasia. It was rumored that Gallo, under orders from Genovese was responsible for the attempted assassination of Frank Costello, head of the Luciano crime family in Manhattan and close ally of Anastasia. The world would be a better place, thought JP, if they would kill each other off.

A race war in the Bronx would dilute their earnings and give Genovese an excuse to get rid of Anastasia, and take over control of the Five Families. No matter what happens, JP mused, we're fucked.

Tanya returned and sat down. Taking her wine she finished her drink and motioned to the waiter for a refill. JP said nothing and waited.

"Louis wasn't home. I called the Hospital and tracked him down in the ICU. I explained to him you're rational behind Cynthia's protection. He said she wouldn't be left alone."

"What else, Tanya?"

"She came out of the coma. She is still unable to concentrate, but the doctor said it was only a matter of time. She recognized her family. She's going to recover!"

Chapter 26

1957—Manhattan

"Thank God she's awake and will recover. However, when she can talk coherently, she will tell Louis who her assailants were, and the shit's going to hit the fan."

"Right now I don't care, JP. All I care about is that she will recover. I just want to shut everything else out for now."

"Does this mean we're calling a truce and we can order a main course?"

"For now."

Approximately an hour later, they were having espresso laced with sambucca, and cannoli's for dessert.

She sat back and looked JP in the eyes, and in a soft voice devoid of anger, she spoke. "Why are you and your people such bigots? What is it that makes you hate anyone who is not white and Italian? Are we so different than you? We didn't ask to be here. Your ancestors stole us from our world and forced indignities upon us that can never be forgiven, and shouldn't be forgiven. Our races will never learn to love one another, but we deserve the same expectations, opportunities, and hopes that you believe belong to you. You try to keep us from your neighborhoods, your schools, your children. You can only do that for so long, JP. You and your kind can't keep us down forever. I don't get it. You obviously possess a much higher IQ than most of your friends, and you're always sure of yourself, and you're street smart. My cousin told me you think you're hot shit because you graduated near the top of your class. You act more like a university graduate than an eighteen-year-old with no future. So tell me, JP. What makes you wallow in the gutter, a bigot and a racist?"

There was a moments silence as JP paused to light a cigarette before answering her.

"You're a beautiful girl, Tanya, and sitting across from you, I don't see in myself those things of which you accuse me. I'm with you because you are beautiful and intelligent, and I enjoy sparring with you. I would love to jump your bones in bed, so yeh, that's one of the reasons I'm with you also, but then so would every guy who looks at you, regardless of race. I personally think your color enhances your beauty, the same way that blue eyes or flawless skin enhances. I want to hold you and kiss you, and just once have you look at me and not think of me as your enemy.

"I grew up in an all-white Italian neighborhood. It was the same neighborhood my grandfather moved to when he came over from the other side. He worked his ass off in the garment district of New York. He put his nine kids through school, and through those years watched his family take abuse, beatings, and harassment from the non-Catholic, non-Italian bastards who resented those guinea monkeys from Italy dirtying up their neighborhood. Our family didn't belong in the North Bronx, according to them. We belonged down here on Mulberry Street and the Bowery with the rest of the unclean immigrants. My uncles came home from school bloodied and beaten some days. They were constantly being taunted by non-Italian children. My aunts were hounded, propositioned, and called pigs and wop whores. But they are a proud people. They wore hand-me-downs from the older siblings, but they not only survived but prospered by their standards. They built a life in the Bronx, and no one was going to take it away from them

"They were taught by their parents there were people different than them who would destroy their way of life. All the hatreds and bigotries they endured were passed to their children. The blacks and Puerto Ricans became low-life people in their eyes. The same epitaphs that were flung at my people they taught their children to use on others. There were people who would try to destroy their way of life. They would bring crime, they were lazy and shiftless, and they would defile our women. Your people weren't *blacks*. You were *niggers*, just as we weren't considered Italians, but wops. Puerto Ricans were spics, and the Irish were micks. Bigotry and hate are taught; they are not hereditary; Growing up, I aligned myself with guys just like me. We had no money. Our baseball bats were broom sticks and our baseballs were Spalding rubber balls. We played in the street and used sewer covers as bases. But our families made sure we never went hungry. Some of our clothes were hand-me-downs, but we always went to school washed and dressed properly.

"I have a lot in common with all those guys on the Avenue. I'm grateful for what my family has done for me, and if they could afford the tuition, they would want me to go to college, but they can't. Everyone in the family works when they're old enough. I look at Sally G and Anastasia and the rest of those hoods and it burns my ass that they throw money around the way they do. But that's why I work for them. I'm not going to deliver vegetables for fifteen cents an hour plus tips, nor am I going to sweep sidewalks for spending money.

"I'm eighteen years old, and I'm bringing in two, three hundred a week running numbers and shy-locking for Sally G, and yeh, sometimes we do other jobs for them. But doing these things I can sit here and spend thirty or forty dollars for a meal. I don't plan to run with a gang much longer, but until I leave I don't want this to end. I just don't want to get caught.

"Some of those guys are never leaving. They'll stay with the mob until they get sent to jail or are found in a vacant lot with a bullet hole in the back of their head. That's the future they settle for. Those that get out are the lucky ones and you're upsetting their world, Tanya. They see the blacks and Puerto Ricans as a threat to them.

"My Grandfather is eighty-five years old. He hears his children speak of blacks and Puerto Ricans as niggers and Spics, blaming them for all their ills in life. He anguishes over it because he knows that he is partially to blame. I know he wishes he could take back the epitaphs he used when he was being wronged by someone of a different color. He took some of that hate and passed on to his children, and they in turn passed on to us. Now I understand what he meant when he told me we inherit the sins of our fathers."

JP sat back looking exhausted. He had never spoken to anyone, pouring his heart out. He felt saddened because he knew he had driven her further away. He sat back and lit a cigarette.

95

"It sounded like you were planning to leave the gang soon," Tanya asked. "Where are you going?"

"Me and one of my close buddies pushed our numbers and are going into the service."

"Pushed your number?"

"We're eligible for the draft. Rather than wait to be called, we requested to be drafted. This way we serve only two years and get it done, rather than wait to be called. I'll be outta' here, choose what I want to do, and be eligible for the GI Bill when I get out. Let them pay for my college education."

She said nothing for a moment. "JP, I love Chinatown and the Soho district. Can we get out of here and walk for a few minutes?"

"Sure but it's going on midnight. You don't have to be home?"

"Let me worry about that."

Chapter 27

1957—Manhattan

Del pulled into the delivery driveway forty-five minutes after leaving White Castle. He backed into the alleyway until the rear of the car was even with the door leading to the kitchen. The restaurant was situated on Mott Street, halfway between Broome and Hester Streets. The storefront was small, the windows streaked with grime, making it impossible to see inside the restaurant. A small unlit sign identified it as Quan Lee's. Any tourists who strayed off the main streets would not think about stopping at this dirty little hole in the wall.

Upon entering the restaurant, a visitor would have been pleasantly surprised by the décor and ambiance. Huge lithographs portraying China's countryside decorated the walls of the large room. The room itself consisted of several rows of booths, the red-leather of the seating complementing the black-lacquered tabletops. Several small rooms were situated on the periphery of the larger room, giving privacy for small parties. The offset lighting gave the area a subdued, intimate feeling.

The clientele consisted overwhelmingly of well-dressed Chinese. Quan Lee catered to those at the top of the political and crime hierarchy in New York. The low murmur of Chinese dialects could be heard over the slight sounds of dishes being served. The menus in this establishment were in Chinese. To further dissuade non-Chinese visitors, the waiters spoke no English. In the rear of the restaurant were the doors leading to the kitchen. In the rear of the kitchen was a locked steel door leading to another large room. This room served as a warehouse and distribution center for the huge amounts of illegal contraband that passed through Chinatown. Leader of the most powerful Tong in the country, Quan Lee supplied New York with drugs, contraband, and prostitutes.

Tony rang the bell, and a moment later the door was opened by one of Quan Lee's soldiers.

"What can I do for you, gentlemen?" He spoke perfect English with a slight accent

"Sally G from the Avenue said you would be expecting us." Tony was somewhat nervous. He knew these hoods would just as soon cut their throats rather than do business with non-oriental's.

The henchman said something in Chinese to someone inside. Two men came out and started to empty the back seat. Del opened the trunk, and the men emptied it of its cargo. After they finished unloading, the Chinese went inside without a word to the boys. Conversation wasn't necessary. Sally G would receive whatever money was coming to him, and he in turn would pay the Berettas.

"Let's leave the car here and go get something to eat. Better yet, let's go over to that titty bar on Broome Street," Tony offered.

"Why not?"

Two streets removed, JP and Tanya exited the restaurant and slowly walked south. They took several steps when JP stopped and looked into Tanya's eyes. She didn't resist when he cupped her face in his hands and kissed her lightly on her lips. She leaned forward and their lips came together again. This time there was urgency in their embrace. Her lips parted to allow his tongue to search for hers. They held each other tight as she buried her head into his shoulder. The heat emanating from his body mingled with the subtle aroma of his aftershave, enveloped her, and drew her into him ever more tightly. JP was oblivious to his surroundings. The traffic noise diminished and the pedestrian traffic that swirled around them dissolved. It was as if they were the only two people left in the world. He kept telling himself she was just another piece of tail, a change of luck, nothing more. He wasn't falling in love with her; she was a black, for Christ's sake, just a good looking nigger. He'll be gone in a few weeks, and probably never see her again. Why did he feel a sense of panic? He didn't want to let her go, yet he knew she would be no good for him. His emotions were on a roller coaster, and he hated her for getting under his skin. She couldn't be in his life. There was no room.

Del and Tony walked up Broome Street heading for the adult supper club. As they passed Baxter Street, Tony saw the couple embracing outside Forlini's. They were going hot and heavy, and his first thoughts were they should get a room. As the couple released their embrace he recognized JP. "What the fuck? . . ."

Del closed his eyes as if to will the image away.

Tanya pushed JP from her forcibly. Tears were streaming down her face, the little makeup she wore leaving a trail through wetness. "What are we doing, JP? Are we crazy? Please! I need to go home now!" She was starting to panic, sobbing uncontrollably. As she turned away from JP, he reached out for her arm. At first she started to struggle to get away from him, and just as suddenly she stopped and just stood there shaking.

"C'mon, I'll take you home, Tanya," he said quietly. "The car is just around the corner in the municipal lot." She didn't resist as he put his arm around her and led her down the street. They never saw Tony and Del watching them.

Chapter 28

1957—Manhattan

Nothing was said as they made their way to the car. He opened the door for her and then walked around the car to the driver's side. She reached across and unlocked the door for him.

"Thanks." He talked quietly to her as he started the car and made his way out of the garage. "I'm not sorry for what just happened, Tanya. I can't help this feeling. I don't understand it myself. I just know that it's different with you. I want to hold you and touch you, and never stop. Please don't say anything about race, or gettin' lucky or the color rubbing off. Don't make what just happened cheap. You just don't understand what I feel." Tanya didn't say a word. They were on the East Side Drive heading north towards Harlem and the Bronx.

JP never felt so bad. He didn't know what to say to make things right. It seemed everything he did or said made the situation worse. A crushing silence hung over them as he made his way north.

She finally slid towards him and spoke. "Get off at 63rd Street. Make a right on York Avenue and pull into the Rockefeller University parking lot. Go to the southeast corner of the lot and park. No one will bother us.

"Just in case you're wondering, I take classes at the university. That's how I know my way around the campus." She was talking quietly, using a tissue from the package sitting on the dashboard to remove her ruined makeup. She was struggling to reclaim control of her emotions. She had to talk to him, tell him what a mistake they were making, but she was filled with conflicting emotions. It was just as much her fault as it was his. She wanted him to kiss her, hold her, and tell her how much he needed her. But she couldn't let it go any further. She had to put an end to it.

Following her directions, he pulled into the lot and parked as she instructed. There were only a few cars in the lot, the night lights giving off a dim glow. He parked in the shadow of a locked delivery truck that was waiting for morning to unload. He turned the engine off, leaving the radio on. They faced one another and kissed lightly. The New York DJ who coined the term 'Rock and Roll' introduced his next song with a smooth enticing tone.

"This is the Moondog, Alan Freed, bringing you the love songs that make you want to snuggle. And now the beautiful sounds of the Platters singing 'Twilight Time.'"

The singer's velvet tones enveloped the two young lovers.

"We can't do this, JP. Do you know how many lives we will be destroying? This is the stupidest mistake we could make."

"Shut up, Tanya," he whispered softly. He tenderly cupped her face with his hands and drew her slowly to him. He kissed her eyes, her face, and her lips. She melted into his touch. He kissed her neck, his lips finding the edge of her blouse where the apex of her firm breasts met. He felt the intake of her breath as his hand slid down her back and unclasped her brassiere as he releasing her breasts. He kissed her face and neck and worked downwards until he was caressing her nipples with his tongue. She wrapped her arms around him and slid into the seat pulling him down with her. He lifted his head and found her lips again. He slid his hand between her legs, and lifted her skirt from her body. He slid his fingers inside her underpants, feeling the silkiness of her pubic hair. Tanya moaned as his fingertips found her cleft, and he started massaging her. Suddenly, she started pushing him away. "Please stop, JP. Please let me get up. This is wrong. Please stop," she said softly. He moved off her and positioned himself on the driver's side of the car. He didn't say a word as he fumbled with his cigarettes, finally getting them out of his pocket. He lit the Camel and leaned against the window. Tanya sat up and straightened her clothes out. She didn't look at him, but just stared out of the window. Her mind was in turmoil, her body on fire. She never wanted anyone as badly as she wanted JP. She wanted his arms around her, his body fused with hers. She knew how wrong it was, and it had nothing to do with morals. He still hadn't said a word. He lit a second cigarette from the first and handed it to her. She laid her head back on the seat, took a drag and closed her eyes as she blew a stream of smoke out.

JP took another drag and looked into her eyes. "I know we're young and we're not supposed to know what we're doing, but nothing seems more right than you and I together. I can't hold you or touch you enough. You have been on my mind since the first time I saw you at the dance. I know you feel the same way. I'm not stupid. I know the consequences, but just once think with your heart and not your mind, Tanya."

She turned towards him and kissed him long and hard, her tongue finding his. She smiled and opened the door

"There's a lot more room in the backseat, JP."

They lay entwined in each other's arms. Her right leg was draped over his left leg, her nakedness pressed against the back of the seat. They were sweating freely, the perspiration sealing them together in their nudity. They coupled frantically, holding on to one another tightly as they shut the world out, forgetting the nightmares that awaited them. They couldn't get enough of each other as they raced towards a climax, never wanting it to end. When it did, they both sat up, still holding on to one another.

"What are we going to do, JP?"

"I don't know, but I won't let you go, Tanya."

"We don't have a choice, JP. We can't be seen together. We have to wait."

JP didn't answer her. He realized the futility of his words to her as he allowed reality to set in—a reality that crushed his hopes of openly sharing their love and being together. Of course he would let her go. A race war was imminent. It would surely drive a wedge between them. Even if their relationship survived, he had the Army waiting for him. They were in a no-win situation. One way or another, this relationship would end; they would move on with their lives.

Tanya disentangled herself and dressed. "Let's go, JP. I have to get home."

Chapter 29

1977—The Bronx

The 47th precinct was fairly quiet. Lieutenant Billy Mongelli sat with his feet propped up on the desk. His leg felt better when he rested it. He stared at the ceiling, his hands clasped together supporting his neck.

The *Daily News* was opened to page six. The small two—paragraph article made note of the fact that a commuter was stabbed to death as he boarded the Lexington Avenue Express at Grand Central station. His name was given as Michael Scarpetta. The perpetrator was not identified. The investigation was ongoing.

He swiveled his chair around and stared at the blackboard he had propped up on another chair. Written on the board in chalk were the names of the Berettas, taken from personnel records he kept over the years. He didn't have all the names, but he had written the names of those he believed were key players in the gang, and who were present that night in the summer of '57.

Johnny (JP) Piscalli
Tony Chicarella
Danny Marconi
Frankie Grazio
Pete 'Satch' Lombardo
Joe Rustico 'Little Tom'   —murdered
Mike Scarpetta   —murdered
Geno Contelmo
Marco Napolitano

Johnny Delgardo

Also listed: Angelo Spedino, Jamey Desego, Benny Coletta, and Chippy Longo, members of a local club dubbed "The Shack Boys". He decided to add one more name, picked up the chalk and wrote "Father Martin—murdered" below the gangbangers names. He sat back and stared at the board, reliving that night twenty years ago.

"Nice to see someone working."

"What the hell?" Mongelli was startled by the voice. He turned around to face FBI Agent Lou Iozzino, a twenty-year vet in law enforcement—five of those years served with the NYPD. His specialty with the FBI was profiling serial killers.

"What's up, Lou?"

"Well to begin with, we just came back from a Signal 5. The victim was found in an alley off Belmont Avenue. The name on his driver's license was Gino Contelmo. Quite a coincidence, considering his name is written on your board and right below two other names with 'murdered' written next to them."

"Sit down, Lou. I have a story to tell you. Let me know if I'm nuts. When I'm done you need to see the Captain and get the OK for you and I to team up on this case."

After Iozzino left and headed for the Captain's office, Mongelli took the chalk and wrote "murdered" next to Contelmo's name.

This is getting weird, he thought. None of the murdered men were affiliated with the mob, nor was there any suspicion they were into the rackets. One had a family and lived in Connecticut. The other had lived in Las Vegas. Contelmo had owned an Italian restaurant on Arthur Avenue in the Bronx. They all had been gainfully employed. But there were other commonalities. They grew up on the Avenue. They belonged to the same gang when they were kids. All left the Avenue after the incident, making themselves scarce. The task force searched for Rustico after that night, but he had dropped below their radar. Twenty years later he shows up dead in a sleazebag hotel in New Orleans. Contelmo was questioned but released. He just kept denying he was there.

Coincidence that the priest ends up murdered also. He believed he was the savior of those gangbangers. He was convinced that the blacks and whites could live in harmony. What a naive bastard.

There is no doubt in my mind that these deaths are related. If I let my imagination run amok, I could believe that one of those men shared a confidentiality with the priest, something that was later regretted. Something the priest might share with the wrong people. Too farfetched! These guys were Catholics. If they were to share some dark forbidden secret, they would do so in the confessional where it would stay; the priest being unable to divulge any conversation between priest and confessor. Maybe we need to rattle a few cages. Find out who Rustico's pals were in Vegas. Maybe he shared some secrets. I think we'll also pay a visit to Scarpetta's wife.

Chapter 30

1977—Manhattan

"I was going to ask you how you were able to get my private number; but, considering your worth, I guess it should be easy. How are you, JP?"

Please let me be cool, she thought. *Why the hell is my heart beating so fast and why I am so nervous? I haven't seen or talked to him since that summer. Why the hell am I feeling this way?*

"Congratulations, Tanya! I always knew you would end up a high-flying designer-type person, creating the perfect wardrobe and winning all kinds of prizes. I guess being the top model in the country and the most prestigious clothes designer in the world, has its perks. Not to mention being on the cover of *Business Week* and ramming your way into the Fortune 500. You should be damn proud of yourself."

That son of a bitch! She thought. Cocky as ever. But why the hell am I getting angry? Why is my stomach in a knot? Why does the room feel as if it's closing in on me? Why the hell do I want to scream? He must hear the tremor in my voice.

JP's hands were sweating. He was using all his will power to act blasé and give the impression he was in control. But as soon as she answered the phone, his heart started beating rapidly, and he felt his mouth go dry. He reached for the pitcher of water, but Del grabbed it and poured JP a glass. JP saw he was smiling. Del looked him in the eyes and whispered softly, "That was lame, really lame." He headed for the door, leaving JP with all his demons. JP downed the glass of water.

"I guess congratulations are in order for you also, JP. It's a long way from the streets of the Bronx. Good thing I'm not a real gambler.

I would have bet the only way of hearing from you would be a post card from Greenhaven Prison. You can't be calling me for money. You obviously are doing well. Are you calling to absolve me of my sins, JP? Perhaps you wish me to absolve you of yours?"

I know I'm crazy, he thought. She hates my guts.

"I called because I want to take you to dinner. I want to celebrate your success. In truth, I just want to see you again."

"After 20 years, you just want to see me again? Why? We have nothing in common, JP. I ran from you because you dragged me into the hell you people created. If I stayed, I would have suffocated and died. In fact, a part of me has died. You remember, JP. Go to Woodlawn Cemetery in the Bronx. If you look hard enough you can see the Lexington Avenue Line from the hill where they are buried." She paused and caught her breath. There was a tremor in her voice when she spoke again. "I'm sorry, JP. Even after all this time, I just don't know who to blame. We knew there was going to be trouble, but, for the life of me, I never knew it was going to become the most horrible nightmare in my life. I live those few days again and again. I'm afraid to see you JP."

"Please listen, Tanya. Maybe seeing me and talking it out may help. You need me as much as I need you. Please see me!"

"Oh God! I don't know what do!"

"Please! Let's start over again. Let's try that first night over again. I'll pick you up at your place at eight o'clock."

"Eight O'clock, JP." She softly replaced the receiver and walked over to the couch. The tears came more freely, the sobs choking her. She folded herself into a fetal position, exhausted and drained. She fell into a fitful sleep and the nightmares returned.

Chapter 31

1957—Fordham Hospital, The Bronx

She opened her eyes. The first person she saw was her brother Louis sitting next to her on bed. She realized he was holding her hand. Cynthia had no idea how long she had been in a coma. She saw the monsters in her dreams. Their faces were branded in her mind as she relived the nightmare, as it all came back to her.

"What time is it, Louis?"

"Hey, kid. How you feelin'?" Before she could answer, Eugene entered the room.

"Louis. I need to talk to you outside now."

"Later, Eugene."

"No, now!"

"I'll be right back, sweetheart."

Eugene closed the door to the room after Louis joined him. "Whats goin' on man?"

"I was downstairs lookin' over some magazines in that little all night gift shop. I spotted Sally G and another one of Anastasia's guns coming into the hospital and heading towards the elevators. They're comin' after her, Louis!"

Louis looked at the clock on the wall. It was 1 a.m. The floor was quiet, the lights were dimmed. There was no one around.

"What the hell we goin' to do, Louis? I ain't packing. We got no weapons. They just as soon shoot you an' me too."

"You tear-ass down the hall yellin' that she stopped breathing. I'm goin' inside and pull the plug on her heart monitor. That should bring some people running."

Louis went back into the room and walked over to the monitor. He could hear Eugene yelling for help. Louis disconnected the wires monitoring her vital signs. He waited until he could hear the medical team making their way down the hall, then restarted the monitoring equipment.

"What are you doing, Louis? Is that Eugene yelling? Oh my God! What's going on?"

"Everything going to be ok, sis. Not to worry."

Less than a minute later the room was filled with bodies, as the doctor on duty and the attending nurses asked Louis to leave the room. Louis walked out into the corridor just as the elevator doors opened. The gunmen stepped off the elevator, saw Louis and Eugene standing outside the room, then noticed the commotion. Sally G stared hard at Louis, smiled, and stepped back into the elevator. Eugene was shaking uncontrollably, perspiration pouring down his face. Louis slumped against the wall, breathing hard.

Five minutes later, the team of doctors and nurses were gone, bitching to one another about faulty equipment.

Louis and Eugene went back into the room. Cynthia looked at Louis. "What happened? Why did they rush in here?"

"Apparently there was an equipment problem. Nothing to worry about."

"Louis, I remember."

"Who was it, Cynthia?"

In the hospital parking lot Sally G lit a cigarette and started the car. He turned to his partner.

"Those niggers think they're smart. The boss is not going to like this."

"You think she told them who did her?"

"Yeh, I think she told them. I think the Avenue is going to blow up, and we're not goin' to be able to stop it. Everybody loses!"

Chapter 32

1957—Manhattan

She made JP drive her to the corner of 50th Street and then used the pay phone to call a gypsy cab to pick her up. She would not allow JP to drive her anywhere near Harlem, particularly at two o'clock in the morning.

The cab dropped her off in front of her house. As she made her way down the foyer, she noticed the light on in the den. She knocked and entered. Peter was sitting behind the desk, one of his many reference books in his hands. He looked up as she entered the room. "It must have been one hell of a date, sis. It's almost 3 a.m."

"Are you taking Dad's place, Peter?"

"Dad's not home. He took Alicia to Uncle James's for a visit. She wanted to spend some time with her cousins. He's going to leave her there for a day or two. He's planning on spending the night and leave for work from there."

"She looks forward to visiting them. Is Alicia aware that Cynthia will not be there?" "She's well aware. She insisted on going anyway."

"I'm going to bed, Peter. See you in the morning." "Tell me about your date. Did you have a good time?"

"I'll tell you about it tomorrow, Peter. I'm very tired."

"It is tomorrow, Tanya. Do you want me to guess who you were with tonight? That disheveled look about you tells me you had a grand time."

"Fuck you, Peter! I'm going to bed!"

"Cynthia remembered, Tanya. She gave up the guys to her brother. She named a couple of the Berettas. Louis went down the Avenue

110

three o'clock this morning. He and Eugene went to the pool room looking for the guys. They're lucky the white boys didn't beat the shit out them and throw them out. I guess they were too stunned to react. Louis was lookin' for JP since he is the leader of the Berettas; but of course, he wasn't there, so he gave an ultimatum to the Beretta's who were there. Give up the guys by tomorrow night or its all—out war. Then they just walked out. It was a fuckin' miracle they weren't beaten to death. But of course you know JP wasn't there. He was with you."

She sat down and placed her hands over her face. She started rocking back and forth, moaning. Peter walked over to her, knelt and took her into his arms. He held her tightly. Neither one said a word for several minutes. "Who did it, Peter?" she whispered.

"It was that blond piece of shit, Tony. There were two of them. The other was that little ratty guy that follows him around."

"JP didn't know, Peter. The last thing he wants is a race war, but the Berettas won't give those guys up to Louis. They can't."

"Tanya, you have put yourself in a world of shit, being with him. You have to distance yourself from JP. He's no different than the others. When it comes to making a choice between you and them, you're going to discover you're just another nigger in their eyes. You need to stay out of the Bronx until this is over."

"I can't do that, Peter. I have to go there and talk to Louis. I want those bastards dead also. He may get those two pieces of shit, but to do so he has to start a race war. In the end he will be lying face down in the gutter. If the white boys don't kill him, Anastasia's goons will hunt him down. His only chance is to go to the police."

"The police? Do you honestly think the police will do anything? Do you think they care about one black girl? They'll throw him out of the station on his ass. Louis has to go after them. He answers to the Egyptian Kings. If they don't take those honkies out, they would lose face with Harlem gangs, who by the way are ready to help the Kings as soon as Louis gives the word. You can't stop this, Tanya. Your relationship with that white gangbanger will end up making you a pariah to your own people. You will have no life, no future."

"I'm going into the Bronx tomorrow, Peter."

Chapter 33

1957—The Bronx

JP double-parked the car in front of the Park Hill, joining the line of double-parked cars that stretched down the Avenue. It was several minutes past two o'clock in the morning. The Avenue was quiet. The sound of the Lexington Avenue Express could be heard faintly, as it pulled into the 233rd Street station, eight streets north. The weak lighting from the train station and the tall lamp posts that dotted the Avenue, reflected off the darkened storefronts. The streets were void of life.

Very few windows in the tenements that lined the side streets showed any light, or signs of activity. In those apartments occupants were returning from working a swing shift or were preparing to work a graveyard shift. Most occupants were slipping into a deep sleep, doors bolted and alarm clocks set.

The pool room was closed, but the Park Hill was still open. The voice of Johnny Mathis singing the haunting lyrics of "Chances Are" floated out of the bar into the street. JP walked in and ordered a drink. Satch and Del were standing by the small picture window that looked out to the Avenue, sipping their drinks. Contelmo, Little Tom, and Mike were sitting in one of the booths. Angie, Benny, and Grazio were playing table shuffleboard. The bar smelled of cigarette smoke and beer. The two fans over the bar did little to dissipate the smoke.

"Ok! What the fuck is going on?" JP asked

"Was she a good lay, JP?" Satch turned from the window. "According to Tony, you and that hot cousin of Louis's were swapping spit in the middle of the street."

Del spoke, "Tony and I were delivering the goods from the job to Quann Lee. We saw you outside Forlini's."

JP responded, "Tony is worse than a washwoman. It's really not anyone's business who I fuck, is it?"

Angie stopped playing shuffleboard and told JP what went down. "I gotta tell you. That nigger is ballsy."

"Was Tony or Danny there?"

Satch ground his cigarette out. "Yeh, JP! They looked scared shitless. They were in the back. When they heard the nigger's voice they hid behind one of the tables. I thought Danny was goin' faint. Under different circumstances it would have really been funny."

"Where are they?"

Angie slid the puck down the table, not bothering to see the results, and turned to JP. "They lit outta here a few minutes after Washington left. They didn't say a word. I wanted a showdown with those black bastards, but I didn't want it to come this way. Washington knows we can't give those two up. I bet he's counting on it. He wants a war, regardless of how this turns out, I'm going to personally kick the living shit out of Tony, and his stooge."

"Washington will probably come after us tomorrow night, if he can gather his people. He won't have any time to gather a large group. He won't want to wait. He wants revenge." Grazio continued. "His people from Harlem will come up by train. They'll probably get off the Lex at 219th Street or Gun hill Road. That's only fifteen blocks from here. That will place them a half mile down the Avenue. They'll walk from there."

Satch spoke up. "He and his boys will probably come down here from the projects by car. They would have to come down 226th Street, or 224th Street to the Avenue because they're one-way streets in our direction."

Marco continued the thought. "Let them come to us. If they do come by car, we can cut off the streets back to the project and trap them. I'll get in touch with the Daggers. Maybe they can take Gun Hill Road."

JP finally spoke. "I'll inform the Club 22 guys, but don't count on them helping. They won't want to piss off the Anastasia people. Anyway, I don't think they'll fight unless one of those niggers takes one of them out by mistake."

Angie smiled. "We can only hope."

"T-They won't be h-here until after dark. I figure around n-nine o'clock, or later." Del theorized.

"H-Have the Debs stake out W-Washington and the b-boys from the p-project. Get Terri and Gracie to p-park their asses in that p-phone booth on L-Laconia and 225th. As s-soon as W-Washington moves t-they can call the p-pool room. One of us will be there to p-pick up the phone. H-Have Annie and Chickie h-hang out at that ice cream p-parlor on Gun-Hill and the Avenue. H-Have them call if something g-goes down a-at that l-location. But w-we have to think about another option. They might w-wait for Friday and make their p-play at the church dance. If there is no m-movement tomorrow night, it w-will definitely go down Friday."

JP nodded his head. "Washington will want to come tomorrow night. His boys will try to talk him out of it, claiming they could get more guys if they wait, and we would be cornered in one place. Let's prepare for them coming either night. We'll know by nine o'clock tomorrow night. If the girls don't see any action, and we get no calls from the other gangs, then we have an extra day to prepare. We can't get the Harlem Redwings to help us. They're too tied into the mob. Hopefully, we'll get a call from one of them giving us a heads up."

"What about Tony and Danny?" Satch asked.

"We'll deal with them after this is over!" JP spit out the words. "I wouldn't give a plug-nickel for their asses. The chances are we may not have to deal with them if Anastasia's guys or the blacks get to them first. Either way they're dead men."

JP yawned. "Let's get together tomorrow night at around seven o'clock in front of the pool room. It's almost three o'clock. They're getting ready to lock up here. I'm goin' home and get some sleep."

"Before you go, JP," Angie spoke, "What about you and that black chick? How you goin' to handle that?"

"There's nothing to handle, Angie. She's not part of the equation."

"If Washington finds you been fuckin' his little cousin, you and her will be world of shit. He'll come after you."

"Let him."

Chapter 34

1957—The Bronx

JP couldn't get to sleep. It was almost four—o'clock; and, although he dozed off briefly, the enormity of what had happened and what was to come forced him awake. He sat up, fumbled for his cigarettes, lit one, and sat at the edge of his bed, allowing in all the thoughts he tried so hard to block out. Although a light drizzle pushed some air into the bedroom window, there was no relief from the summer heat. He was perspiring profusely.

He could smell the lingering scent of her perfume, the musky scent of her body, the softness of her breasts. He could still taste her lips, her breasts, and her stomach. He continued downwards burying his face in the pubic hair until his tongue found her labia. He remembered fumbling for his pants and struggling to get the condom from his pocket. When he finally removed it, she took it from him, removed the wrapper, and rolled it over his penis. Their love making was frantic as they both climaxed. They had held on to each other, afraid to let go, knowing the reality they shut out would return.

He kept telling himself he wasn't in love with her. She was just a fantastic lay. But he realized he was fooling himself; he did love her. She had to feel the same way. She kept repeating the words again and again. He could not believe it was said in the heat of the moment. But he also knew he could never be with her openly She did not fit into his plans. He would hold onto her until he entered the service and take what he could from her. He would keep in touch with her while serving and when he returned he would carry on a covert affair with her while he pursued his goals.

His mind returned to the present. He lit another cigarette from the first and focused his thoughts on the coming days. He was sure it would come to a head tomorrow. There was no doubt in his mind that Washington's state of mind would push him into a fight before he was ready. He wanted the blood of the guys who violated his sister, and he wouldn't wait. The Berettas couldn't give Tony and Danny up. If they did, they would become the target of every white gang in the city. Reluctantly, they would have to protect those two despicable bastards until this was over. Then all bets were off, and they would go down, not by the blacks, but by the whites. What the fuck were they thinking?

The Harlem niggers would come up by subway. They would be armed with knives and billy clubs. No bats. Too big and bulky. Probably a few guns if they have them. The boys from the projects will come down to the Avenue armed: bats, guns, and knives. Washington and his sidekicks will definitely be packing. JP reached into his end table and removed the locked jewelry box. Unlocking it, he removed the .25-caliber Beretta Bantam. He released the magazine and checked the eight—round clip. Should he bring it tomorrow night? The fucking risks were monumental. If he got caught with the piece, he would be going to jail instead of the Army. He could always get rid of it if the cops showed up. They couldn't trace it to him.

Last year a couple of the boys did a job for Anastasia which robbing and trashing an Army and Navy store. During the trashing, they came across a crate hidden in the cellar of the store. It contained twenty-four brand-spanking new Beretta Bantams. They took the crate, said nothing to the mob, and sold most of them to other gangs, keeping a few for the Berettas. He had only fired the pistol a few times, the last time about eight months ago when they took a ride upstate to Dutchess county deep into farm country. He spent a box of ammunition in the small backwoods firing range until the gun felt comfortable.

He wasn't sure he had the balls to use it against another human. The gun was small enough to fit in his back pocket. He just didn't want to get caught with it, but he would be a fool not to carry it.

Chapter 35

1957—The Bronx

A few hours earlier than the meeting the Berettas held, a similar type meeting was taking place in the Community Center in Edenwald Projects. Twelve Egyptian Kings were debating when to go after the two Berettas. The general consensus was to wait until they gathered all the manpower available. Washington knew it would take a few days to get all the gangs from Harlem to agree on a time frame. Claude and Eugene knew Washington would not accept the wait.

"If we wait, we'll lose the element of surprise," Washington argued. "Also, it will give them time to bring in the Golden Guineas and the Fordham Daggers. It will also give them time to hide those two motherfuckers, Chicarella and Marconi. I say we move in fast with what we got. We recruit as many brothers from Harlem as we can. They can jump on the uptown Lex after dark and get off at 219th Street, one station south of 225th. Tell them to leave their wheels at home. These streets will only confuse them; they could be easily trapped not knowing the turf.

"We'll come down 224th Street. It's a one-way towards the Avenue, so there will be no cars comin' at us. The Lex should be running on time, so we figure when the train will hit 219th Street and be ready to hit the Avenue at same time as the boys from Harlem. We storm the poolroom, put down anyone in our way, destroy their wheels, and trash the poolroom and the bar. Once we take care of business, we get out before they know what's happening. I intend to blow away those two bastards, and I won't hesitate to put anyone else down who gets in my way."

Several of the gang started talking. Claude rose up from his chair and whistled. They went silent as he voiced his thoughts.

"They're not stupid, Louis. They are goin' to be watching for us. If they find they're outnumbered, they will split and wait until they have enough guys. Some of those guys pack. Also, the moment we step foot in that pool-hall, the manager will call the cops. They'll be on us faster than stink on shit. Let's wait until Friday night. It's only two days off. We'll catch them at the church hall. They'll be together in one place. We would have them trapped. They wouldn't expect us to take them on at the church. They won't have help and won't be prepared for a beef."

Washington stopped pacing. "What about that cop that hangs out there? You think he's goin' to stand by and watch me off some white boys? I'll be packin' my Tauras-94, and it will have a full nine-round load."

"We'll get them out of the church hall and take them down. They won't know what hit them. By the time they recover, we'll be done and outta there. Besides, it's only half a block from the Gun-Hill Station to the church. The boys from Harlem won't have very far to travel. We'll ask them to take care of the cop. If the priest tries to interfere, we'll just knock him on his ass."

Louis shook his head. "You're forgetting the police cruisers that are parked in front of the church. At the first hint of trouble, they'll have the place crawling with bulls. Three days is too long. Today is Tuesday. We hit them Thursday on the Avenue. We can't give them fuckers time to circle the wagons. Tomorrow we rally the Manhattan and Brooklyn gangs. Godamnit! We are going Thursday if I have to go on my own. Just remember those two low life motherfuckers are mine. Claude, get in touch with the Harlem boys and coordinate with them. We'll hit the Avenue around nine o'clock. Let the boys know, so they can time their trip. We're goin' to set this white trash, honky neighborhood on its ass. After we're finished kickin' their asses, we trash that pool hall and bar. Let them know the Avenue belongs to us."

Chapter 36

1957—The Bronx

It was only eleven o'clock in the morning. The heat was shimmering off the blacktop, sending small ripples upwards from the pavement. The stifling humidity was a harbinger of more wet weather.

It was a short walk to Southern Blvd, but she was perspiring freely even in shorts and a tube top. Tanya could feel the warmth through her sandals as she came to the bus stop several minutes before the bus came into view. This bus would take her to Pelham Parkway where she would transfer to another bus that would drop her off at 229th Street and Schieffelin Avenue, a few minutes' walk to the projects. Her eyes, hidden by the large sunglasses she wore, were red rimmed from crying.

She had just left the hospital after spending the last hour with Cynthia and her mother. The shock of seeing Cynthia, her head wrapped in gauze and tape, and her arm in a cast, brought a flood of tears to her eyes. The constant beep of the heart monitor and the IV snaking out of her arm were almost more than she could bear. That she was awake and conversed easily was a tribute to her perseverance.

Cynthia's mother excused herself, taking a much needed break. "Don't leave her for one moment, Tanya, you understand?"

"I promise, Aunt Felice."

After she left the room, Cynthia reached over and grasped Tanya's hand.

"They wanted me dead, Tanya. What kind of monsters are they? What did I ever do to them? Look at me, Tanya. I'll never be pretty again. They ripped my clothes off, and then they . . . they hurt me, again and again. They took turns raping and punching me until I passed out."

"They'll pay for it, Cynthia. They will not hurt you again."

"Louis said he would kill them. They would die for what they did to me. I don't want them to die. If Louis kills them, he'll go to jail for the rest of his life. I just want them to be punished. Louis said, if we depended on the Police, there would be no justice. Please talk to him, Tanya. You're smart. You can talk some sense into him. Please don't let him go down because of me. I'll never forgive myself."

Tanya became angry. "What the hell are you talking about, Cynthia? Forgive yourself! You want to be forgiven for being raped and beaten by a couple of animals. They deserve what's going to happen to them. They *should* die!"

*   *   *

Tanya transferred buses at Pelham Parkway and, a short time later, caught the bus that would take her to the Edenwald Projects. She was oblivious to the stares she received from the males on the bus, as she was accustomed to the looks of admiration.

She couldn't understand the gamut of emotions she was going through. One moment she hated all whites, condemning them to hell and wishing them to die. But then her thoughts turned to JP, and she remembered his touch, his love. Yes, his love. He did love her! It wasn't just sex. They couldn't get close enough; they couldn't hold each other tight enough. She thought of his lips on her face, her neck, and his kisses trailing down her stomach. But then her thoughts turned to her cousin—beaten, raped, and brutalized by the same type of person she lay with a few hours ago in the back seat of a car.

What kind of person was she? What was she to do? It wasn't JP who brutalized her cousin. It wasn't JP that raped her. But he was one of them. He belonged to that cadre of monsters who thought blacks were animals, to be treated as garbage, and to be used as white people saw fit. She was seventeen years old. She knew nothing of love, but if what she was going through was any indication of what it was like, she hated the feeling.

It was Thursday morning. Her aunt was working. Her uncle was off and would be fussing over Alicia all day. I would have time to talk to Louis, to reason with him Tanya thought—hopefully to stop him from destroying his life.

Her thoughts went to JP, damn him! How could she get herself mixed up with him? She didn't understand this love-hate relationship she was going through. Would he be at the church gym Friday night? Would Louis and the Egyptian Kings deal with the Berettas? She had a tremendous foreboding, knowing in her heart this conflict would end badly. She was aware Louis and a few of the Kings had guns. Eugene trying to impress her brandished his pistol one night, while hanging at the Community Center. The Kings would come to this fight armed.

Chapter 37

1977—The Bronx

"OK, Lou. Let's see where we are. We have three old gangbangers murdered. What they had in common was their relationship twenty years ago. They grew up in the same neighborhood and belonged to the same gang. From what we can gather, they parted ways in 1957 and have not kept in touch as far as we know. Scarpetta was married. His wife still lives in Fairfield. Let's start with her."

Less than an hour later, Iozzino and Mongelli were standing at the door of a beautiful stone Tudor home. The seventy-foot driveway leading up to the house was lined with rhododendrons bursting with color. The lawn was immaculate and was being tended by the landscapers, whose truck was parked in the driveway behind a Cadillac. In front of the Cadillac was a fully restored fire engine red '57 Chevy Impala ragtop. The spare tire off the rear bumper was covered with a black boot with the letter "S" imprinted on it in red. Two bicycles were lying on their sides next to the cars.

The two detectives parked in back of the landscaper's truck and made their way to the front door.

Gina Scarpetta was a petite slim brunette. Her olive complexion and dark eyes brought out her Mediterranean heritage. She was wearing denim shorts and a tube top, her hair worn in a ponytail. The dark circles under her eyes broadcast her grief. She identified the two men as law officers immediately.

"Can I see some identification, please?"

The detectives showed her their badges and ID cards.

"You're wasting your time. I don't know any more than I did when I was last questioned. I have no idea why my husband was singled out by the son-of-a-bitch who stabbed him."

Iozzino spoke. "We understand, Mrs. Scarpetta, but all we're asking is a few minutes of your time. We just have a few questions".

With a defeated look on her face, she turned and waved them into the house. "Please, have a seat in the living room. Can I get you something to drink?"

"No thank you, Ma'am." The two detectives sat on the couch while Mrs. Scarpetta sat across from them, in one of the two armchairs.

"Please call me Gina. My children are at friends, and I have to leave in a few minutes to meet with our financial people, so can we be brief?"

"Of course," Mongelli started. "What we really want to talk about is the incident that occurred on the Avenue twenty years ago. We understand it was a long time ago, but perhaps you might help. You're aware that Father Martin was killed a short time ago."

"You believe my husband's murder is related to the killing of Father Martin? What would one have to do with the other?"

"Are you aware that Gino Contelmo and Joe Rustico were also murdered recently?"

"No, I did not know. We haven't seen or talked to any of the old gang since the race incident. I don't speak or communicate with any of the Berettas, except for Johnny Delgardo's wife occasionally. She called to express her sympathy. We were both Beretta Debs and were close when we were young. But even she hasn't gotten in touch with me regarding the murders of Contelmo and Rustico. You think they are all related?" She showed no remorse over the death of the gangbangers.

Lou spoke. "We don't know anything for sure. It just seems that the common thread goes back to 1957. According to our records, your husband was questioned following that night and denied having a part in the altercations. None of the Beretta Debs were questioned, although there was a suspicion they had a part in the incident."

"I don't know anything about that, and if you think I'm going to tell you some enlightening tale about my husband's involvement, you're way off base. The only people I know that were involved were

Tony Chicarella and Danny Marconi. Their actions triggered that horrible night. There's nothing else to tell."

"We are not trying to tie your husband into anything at this time, Mrs. Scarpetta. Is there anything else you can remember about that night that may be able to help us? Anything at all?"

"I will tell you this, but if you involve me in any way I will deny it. The next day when I saw Mike, he was furious. He said that Tony and Danny were dead men, and they deserved it. What pissed him off was that JP was probably going to walk, and he was just as responsible for the outbreak as Tony and Danny. He said that JP's involvement with Tanya Reinford just added fuel to the fire."

Lou and Billy traded glances. "What do you mean?" Lou asked.

"JP was fucking Washington's cousin. You know who I'm talking about. She's that beautiful black girl whose picture is in all the magazines. Mike said the black guys were furious over the relationship, and they wanted JP's ass, as well as Tony's and Danny's. Mike said that JP was with her the night the fight went down. Instead of being there with the boys, he was with that bitch! Two days later Mike told me that she was seen by Satch goin' into the church. Satch figured something was going on and followed her. He saw her talking to Father Martin. What the fuck was she doing in that church?"

"Was anyone with her?"

"I don't know. Why don't you ask Satch? He probably knows more about what went down those days, following that fuckin madness, than anyone else. Or better yet, why don't you go after JP for your answers? Or that black bitch. Perhaps they're too high up in the food chain to bother"

"Thanks for your time, Mrs. Scarpetta. Here's my card. If you think of anything else, please call me." Mongelli handed her the card and walked to the door, Lou following.

Gina Scarpetta stared at the card as if trying to memorize it. She called out as they were making their way down the walk. "Detective Mongelli, wait a moment." Both detectives stopped and turned.

"I remember you now. You used to moonlight at the church on Friday nights when the kids gathered to dance. You were shot that night! The night the blacks came up from Harlem."

"Guilty as charged, Mrs. Scarpetta."

"When I read about it, I felt so bad. You were one of the few cops that tried to keep the peace, except when the blacks showed up and ruined everything. You never took sides. There was no reason for that boy to shoot you."

"Funny thing, Mrs. Scarpetta, he can't tell me why, because he's dead."

Her eyes averted his and she looked away.

"Contelmo's girl at the time was Gracie DeLuzio. Joe Rustico was going with Maria Pisciotta. Gracie married Contelmo and Maria married Joe. If you wait a moment, I'll get their addresses. I don't know if it will do any good. The police never bothered to question the Debs, because the girls made sure they couldn't be found. It was as if we didn't exist. Maybe they'll talk to you now."

Chapter 38

1977—The Bronx

It was agreed upon Iozzino would visit Mrs. Rustico, and Mongelli would visit Mrs. Contelmo to determine if the two women might remember anything that might help in their pursuit of the killer or killers. Iozzino would then proceed to Tanya Reinford's office without giving her notice. Mongelli would do the same with JP. It might stir things up a bit.

After the conversation with Mrs. Scarpetta, Iozzino and Mongelli compared notes.

"Where were JP and Tanya that night, Billy? Do you recall if they were seen or picked up by the police?"

"I don't recall their names coming up in the case files. Obviously I was out of the loop because of being wounded, so I couldn't follow up. Besides, I was concentrating on how I was bushwhacked that night. I really would like to know what happened. When they found me I was unconscious, and the perp was lying there dead with multiple stab wounds, the gun by his side. That case is still open. No one really cared. All that mattered was the perp who shot me paid with his life."

Mongelli dropped Lou off at his car. They would compare notes again, after the visits. Calls to the offices of JP and Reinford confirmed they were both at work.

On his way over to JP's office, Mongelli went over his conversation with Gracie Contelmo. Although separated from her husband at the time of his murder, she was left fairly well off but continued to work, commuting to Manhattan from her condominium located within the bedroom community of Yonkers. They had no children, and during the conversation with her, it came out that she was dating. She was tall and slim, dressed in skin tight jeans and a halter top that highlighted her ample breasts. Her naturally long blond hair hung loose around her shoulders. She wore little lipstick or makeup. Even without the makeup, she was a striking woman. She seemed nervous and edgy, and continually asked why she was being questioned. No, she didn't know why he was killed or who might have done it, but she didn't care. "Let me tell you something, Lieutenant, he was a miserable tortured human being who paid for his sins"

"Do you think his death was related to that night in 1957?"

Her eyes flooded with tears. "You have no idea the misery and torture he caused so many people. He deserved to die."

She wouldn't elaborate and refused to answer any more questions, asking the lieutenant to leave.

"You're holding something back, Mrs. Contelmo. What is it? What do you know that you're not telling me? If you're withholding information, you can find yourself in serious trouble."

"Please leave. I have nothing more to say."

"Here's my card. I suggest you think long and hard about what you're doing. I'll be in touch."

He left the house and went to his car. He sat behind the wheel without starting the car. He saw her staring at him through the kitchen window. She appeared to be crying.

She knows why he died, Mongelli mused, *and she has a good idea who is behind these killings. I'll talk to Iozzino. We have to brace her, push her to talk before someone else dies.*

It was already too late.

Grace Contelmo watched Lieutenant Mongelli drive away. Tears were flowing freely, and she couldn't stop sobbing. She was responsible for the deaths. She set off this horrible chain of events with the letter she had written. But they deserved to be punished for their crime. She wrote the letter asking forgiveness for her husband's treachery; instead, she put into motion a trail of death, only adding more victims to those that died on that day, twenty years ago.

Chapter 39

1977—The Bronx

Marco Napolitano was a numbers runner and shylock for the Anastasia family. As a shylock, he loaned the mob's money out to whoever needed a fast loan and could not get credit anywhere else. For every five dollars he loaned out, he received six back. If not paid back in one week, it cost the borrower seven dollars. If the total amount could not be paid back on time, the borrower was allowed to pay back just the interest on the loan. It was a lucrative business for the mob, and Marco earned ten percent on all interest. Not to pay back any amount was looked upon with great disdain by the mob, and the borrower usually ended up with broken bones or worse. Marco also received ten percent of the numbers money he collected each day. He was also a gopher for the mob, doing odd jobs and errands.

Today he was on his way to Chinatown to collect from Quan Lee; monies owed the mob for goods delivered. Quan was still the fence for the mob even though he was nearing eighty years old.

The doors to the Lexington Avenue express opened with a hiss and Marco entered and sat. Being so close to the beginning of the Lexington Avenue run, there was no problem in finding a seat on the train. He chose one at the end of the car with his back to the wall. He could scrutinize the entire car from where he sat. He enjoyed people watching, and it made the hour long ride tolerable.

As the train entered the tunnel at 149th Street and made its way downtown, the cars began to get more crowded. By the time the train pulled into Mott Street, there was standing room only. Marco elbowed his way to the door as the train pulled into the station. Several people were pushing their way out the door when it opened. He felt the incredibly sharp pain in his upper back as his heart began to burst in his chest. He turned and looked into the eyes of his assailant. As he started to fall, the killer propped him up against the closing door, the other passengers oblivious to what was happening. "You know me, don't you, Marco? Say goodbye."

He fell to the floor, the doors constantly hitting against his dead body as they tried to close.

Typical of New York, commuters simply walked around or over him. They were very annoyed by the delay caused by the doors being unable to close.

Chapter 40

1957—The Bronx

JP was in the Park Hill sipping on a Dewar's and soda. He was leaning against the picture window looking out to the Avenue and the stairs leading up to the train platform. He watched as commuters made their way up and down the stairs.

Every fifteen minutes a train pulled into the station serving commuters entering and leaving the seven-car train. Coming off the train, the commuters melded with the light crowd of people taking care of their business on the Avenue. The stores were doing a brisk business catering to shoppers.

Although mostly white, there were a substantial number of black and Hispanic people shopping the Avenue. Times are changing, thought JP, as he watched the shoppers make their way around the cliques of young people hanging out.

Even though the gangbangers blocked the sidewalk in front of the shops, nothing was said to them. The shoppers made their way around them, not making eye contact. The shopkeepers knew better than to attempt to chase the boys. They valued their businesses too much.

The young women, who were not associated with the gangbangers, crossed the street or quickly hurried by the groups, not wanting to take the verbal abuse thrown at them.

Although there was metered parking along the Avenue most of the guys double-parked. JP noted there were at least six cars doubled-parked, several of them with their radios blasting. Even though he was inside the bar, he could hear Wolfman Jack introducing the Platters latest song, "I'm Sorry".

He spotted Del leaning against his '49 Ford convertible, his arms around his girl, Annie. A few of the other Berettas and some of the Shack Boys were milling around.

None of them seemed too concerned about the upcoming confrontation with the Kings. Where and when? How many? On their side, the Daggers committed ten and the Guineas twelve. The multi-generational Fordham Baldies offered help if it was needed. Between the Berettas and the Shack Boys, there was at least twenty. But we need the time frame, thought JP.

"Hey, JP," Albe, the owner and bartender called him. "Phone call."

"Thanks, Albe". JP picked up the phone. "JP, this is Jimmy Pope. You remember me. You did me a favor last year when you introduced me to Chickie at Orchard Beach. Great broad. I felt I owe you one."

"What's up?"

"You know I live in the Italian section of Harlem. I'm with the Wings."

Italian Harlem was located in Manhattan's eastside between 96th Street and 125th Street and from Lexington Avenue to the East River. It known as one of New York City's "Little Italys".

During the '50s and early '60s, an Italian street gang known as the Harlem Redwings controlled this turf.

"We have no skin in the beef you're getting into, but I felt I owed you. According to our eyes down here in Harlem, something big is going down Thursday. There's talk about raiding your turf. What's scary is the Kings teamed up with one of the Spanish gangs from here. They're coming up by car and train. They plan on meeting down here at about 7:30."

"Appreciate the heads up, Jimmy. We really needed that information."

"No Problem. I would appreciate it if you keep the source to yourself. We don't have too good a relationship with the Baldies or the Daggers, and my guys might get pissed at me for helping you out."

"Not a problem, Jimmy. Thanks again."

JP hung up and ordered another scotch. He knew where, when, and how many. He would meet with the guys and form a strategy. Missing was the Kings plan on how they would approach the Avenue from the Edenwald Projects. I need to make a phone call.

*   *   *

Tanya picked up the phone. "This is Tanya."

"I need to see you tonight. Please say you'll meet me."

Her heart was racing. Her mind told her to say no, but her heart prevailed. "I'll meet you at 9 o'clock. Pick me up two blocks south of my street; there is a small supermarket there. I'll be in front."

JP got in his Ford Fairlane and headed for the East Side Drive. After JP left the Park Hill, Scarpetta turned to Del. "He's meeting that nigger broad, isn't he?"

"It's none of my fuckin' business Mike. It's also none of yours." Del could see the guys were pissed.

"Listen, we don't know how the Kings are going to come at us. Maybe he's trying to find out."

Scarpetta sneered. "Meanwhile it's ok to fuck the broad even though she's a nigger, while we get crucified for having a little fun."

"You and your asshole buddy raped and beat a girl and left her for dead. The only reason you're still here is because we need the headcount, but no matter what happens you're dead meat."

"I'll take care of myself. But JP isn't helping. He's just stoking the coals."

*   *   *

They were back in Rockefeller University, parked in the deep recesses of the parking Lot. They lay in the back seat of the Fairlane tangled in each other's arms. Perspiration clung to their naked bodies. JP disentangled himself and reached over to start the engine. The cold air from the air conditioner reached them in the backseat cooling their bodies. Neither spoke for a time. She turned to JP. "I can't continue this, JP; it's destroying me. I'm in trouble with my family and friends over this relationship. Every time we talk or see one another, someone finds out. Last night Claude called me. He said he was going to kill you on sight, and if I was caught with you again he would make me pay. They hate me for what I'm doing."

"Fuck them. I swear no one will touch you. I'm leaving in a couple of weeks. That will give you two years to decide if you want to spend the rest of your life with me."

"And when you come out, what are you going to do? Run numbers, shylock, and steal for a living?"

"That's not going to happen. I hate those guys as much as I hate those people tearing us apart."

"By those people you mean us blacks."

"You're twisting my words. I don't care about them. All I care about is you. Let me tell you what I think of the mob.

"Last year I needed cash to buy this car. Sally G slipped one night and was mouthing off about a hood that worked for Anastasia, name of Michael Cappola. He collected numbers money from us runners; and once a week he would deliver it to Anastasia, who in turn split it with the five families. By the end of a week he would have in his possession approximately fifty-thousand dollars to be delivered to the bosses.

"Cappola lived in a tenement on 227th Street on the third floor. I got together with Contelmo and Little Tom. If we got into his apartment when he wasn't there, we could find the money and take a couple of grand. No one would be the wiser. We watched the apartment for a couple of days. We knew the fire escape window to the bedroom was always locked, but the second bedroom window about three feet from the fire escape was always cracked to let in the air. To get to that window you had to inch along the ledge that extended out about four inches.

"Several days after we cased the apartment, he took an overnight trip to Atlantic City. That night we climbed up the fire escape to his floor. I hopped over the fire escape railing and inched my way across the ledge to the other window. I entered the room, walked over to the fire escape window, and let the guys into the apartment.

"It took us all of five minutes to discover the dresser drawer with the money. There were stacks of bills wrapped in rubber bands. We decided to take three of the stacks and left the same way we came in. I locked the window behind the guys, and I went out the other window across the ledge to the fire escape. We never told anyone. We netted three thousand dollars, one thousand each. We stowed the money and didn't touch it for several months. We never knew what happened, or if he knew he was robbed."

"You stole all that money. That makes you a common thief, JP."

"We just took money from crooks, Tanya. If they found out they would have killed us, but they didn't, and I have my Fairlane."

She didn't say anything. She knew they could never be together, and she was sad. She loved him, but he represented everything alien to her. She knew firmly she would never have a life with him.

"JP, I think I have to get back. I'm frightened for what going to happen in the next few days. The Kings are planning to come at you from Edenwald on foot and with cars blocking the streets. You know they're also bringing people from Harlem."

"Make sure you stay home, Tanya. Make sure your family doesn't go out."

She reached over to her purse and handed him a small box. Opening it he found a small medal on a chain. "It's Saint Jude. He's the patron saint of lost causes. Wear it so you will think of me when we're apart."

"I'll be wearing it every day. I'll give it back when I return from Army. I promise you, we are not a lost cause. You'll always be in my life."

Chapter 41

1977—Manhattan

"You have a visitor." Adele informed JP when he answered the intercom. "A Lieutenant Mongelli. He doesn't have an appointment. I'll make an appointment for him at a later time if you are predisposed at the moment."

"No, that's fine, Adele. I have about twenty minutes before my next meeting. Besides, I'm very curious. It isn't every day one gets a visit from one of New York's Finest."

JP greeted Mongelli when he entered and led him to a chair facing the desk. JP walked around the desk and sat down facing the police officer.

Mongelli took note that the visitor's chair seemed to be lower than JP's. He remembered reading somewhere this scenario was meant to intimidate the visitor, and therefore put him on the defensive.

"I hope you don't mind, Mr.Piscalli, my damn hemorrhoids are killing me. I prefer the couch."

"Of course. I'll join you."

I need to be really careful with this guy, JP thought, as he made his way to the opposite end of the couch.

Adele set the timer on her desk for twenty minutes. That's all the time allowed for this visit. She had her orders. She shook her head and smiling, went back to her chores.

"What can I do for you, Detective Mongelli? I don't want to be rude, but just to let you know, I only have twenty minutes."

"It's Lieutenant Mongelli, and hopefully my visit won't take twenty minutes. I have a few questions if you don't mind".

"Please get to it."

"I wonder if your CFO John Delgardo might join us."

"Mr. Delgardo is in San Francisco at the moment. He won't be back until Monday. Now, can you tell me what this is about, Lieutenant?"

"I'm sure you are aware of the murders of your childhood friends that occurred over the last several months. You were a member of the same gang, the Italian Berettas, were you not?"

"Yes, I'm aware of them. We were members of the same Social Club, but aside from Johnny, I have completely lost touch with the others. I was sorry to hear about their sudden demise, and obviously I'm somewhat concerned. If you're worried about the safety of Johnny and me, rest assured we have plenty of protection. I honestly believe their deaths probably had something to do with their endeavors later in life, and are not related to that time we spent as friends. Have you determined if they had common interests in the last few years?"

"It seems that like yourself, they had distanced themselves from each other. It is almost as if they purposely sought to avoid any contact.

"So you or Mr. Delgardo wouldn't have any idea who might be the perpetrator. You don't know of any common enemies they had? Perhaps some fallout from the old days when you were gangbangers, hanging out on the Avenue?"

"We were hardly gangbangers, and no, I can't help you there, Lieutenant."

"I would like to change the subject for a moment, Mr. Piscalli. Do you personally know Tanya Reinford?"

Although JP tried not to change his demeanor, the lieutenant watched him struggle to keep his composure.

"Everyone knows who Tanya Reinford is, Lieutenant. You would have to be from another planet not to recognize her name."

"That's not what I asked, sir. I asked if you know her personally."

"As a matter of fact, I did know her. We were friends twenty years ago, but until yesterday, I hadn't seen or spoken to her in all those years."

"Yesterday?"

"Yes, I saw her picture on the cover of *Business Week*. I called to congratulate her on her success."

"Mr. Piscalli, when talking to several of the people you were close to in 1957, all were fairly adamant that you and Miss Reinford were having an affair."

"Lieutenant, any relationship that I had with Ms. Reinford in 1957 ended that year. Why are you asking me questions about events that occurred twenty years ago? What's this have to do with the murder of some ex-friends?"

"I believe they are related, that the incident which occurred in 1957 triggered the recent murders. Can you remember where you were the night of the race altercation? The people I talked to the last few days said you were not seen that night. Considering you were the unofficial leader of the Beretta's, you seemed to have been conspicuously missing from the Avenue. Were you with Ms. Reinford? If so, where were you?"

"I think that's enough, Lieutenant. I have an appointment, so you will have to excuse me. In the future if you have any questions, please call my lawyer."

"Thanks for your time, Mr. Pascalli. I will be getting back to you, so I suggest you alert your legal people."

Chapter 42

1977—The Bronx

Mongelli met Iozzino back in his office, in the 47th. The lieutenant filled Lou in on his meeting with JP.

"There's no doubt he is keeping something from us. I think the killings are related to that race riot back in '57. I also believe JP or Tanya Reinford can give us the link. You couldn't get to her, Lou? What happened?"

"I think she was warned before I got to her office. Her secretary was adamant, saying Reinford would not be available in the foreseeable future. What happened twenty years ago that would trigger these murders? Do you think the shooting incident involving you is a link to these killings?"

Mongelli sat back and closed his eyes, the memory of that night flooding his mind.

"I think about it often. I was on foot patrol, heading east on 225th Street near the elementary school, P.S.21. I was following a couple of gangbangers who were heading east towards the projects. The fighting already started on the Avenue in front of the poolroom.

"Two patrol Cars came on the scene. Several of the black kids broke away from the fight and headed up 225th, so I went after them. As they passed under the street light, I recognized one of the kids. He split off from the group he was with and cut across the street towards the back of the school. Under the light it looked like he was carrying a weapon. He was running towards 226th Street. Because I thought he was carrying, I went after him.

"He stopped and began conversing with someone I couldn't see. The building was blocking my view. I saw him raising the gun, and I yelled to distract him. He turned, and as I was unholstering my weapon, he fired. I went down. It's the last thing I remember until I woke up in the hospital.

"I was told the perp was dead. He was still holding the gun but he had been stabbed, and was dead before they found me. We never found out who stabbed him, obviously the person or persons he had been arguing with, and was getting ready to shoot. It was deduced that my yelling distracted him and gave his potential victim an opportunity to knife him. The investigators chalked it up to a gangbang slaying and forgot about it."

"I think we have to find as many of the Avenue boys as we can and start asking some questions about that night. Apparently the local politicians and your superiors at the time just wanted the incident to go away. Well, it looks like it just came back to haunt them." Lou offered.

"I think you're right, Lou."

"I think we should track down some of the other players and have a talk with them."

Chapter 43

1977—Manhattan

"Mr. Pascalli, Tanya Reinford is returning your call."

"Thanks, Adele."

Tanya started speaking as soon as JP answered.

"A Detective Iozzino was standing outside my office when you called. I sent him away. What's going on, JP?"

"He asked me questions relating to that night." JP filled Tanya in regards to his meeting with the lieutenant."

"Oh God, JP!"

"I don't want to talk over the phone, Tanya. Can we get together for lunch? I can't wait until tonight."

"I have a photo op in two hours. I'll order lunch in. You can come over here." Tanya hung up, fell back in her chair and started to shake. The famous model began to nervously rock back and forth, whispering to herself over and over, *What have I done? What have I done?* She got up and went to her private restroom. Looking at her image in the mirror, she despised what she saw. She pulled herself together and reapplied her makeup.

JP arrived a few minutes after one o'clock.

"We need to tell him we were together that night, JP."

Finished with their catered lunch, they were sipping on coffee when Tanya breached the subject. JP could hear the slight hitch in her voice, knowing she was struggling to stay calm.

"We can, and we will. Here's what we tell the cops. Del and I were cruisin' the streets up near Laconia Avenue trying to determine how many Kings were making their way west to the Avenue. We spotted you near Bronxwood Avenue walking in that direction. We stopped you, and after a prolonged debate, we took you back to the Edenwald Projects and dropped you off at your cousin's. By the time we got back to the Avenue the fight was breaking up. The crew just missed me in the confusion."

"No, JP. No more lying, no more stories. We have to tell the truth! I'm tired of living with this nightmare."

"Nothing good will come from you rehashing that night. We need to put it behind us. Look at us! Both of us are successes in our respective fields. We're admired and respected. You want to throw that away, over something you can never change? Let it go."

"But I killed him. I killed Claude."

"He was going to kill us. You had no choice. It was self defense, Tanya. I have thought about us often, and I was hoping we could start over. We loved each other at one time, but hate and bigotry forced us apart. It's a different world now. We have a chance."

"I thought about that also, JP, but the bigotry and hatred will always be there. Part of it will be carried by people like you and Del and the rest of those gangbangers that meant so much to you. My sister and my uncle are gone. People I love died horribly because of bigots and racists like you. Please go JP."

"If you come out with the truth Tanya, you will destroy everyone close to you, and destroy the better world you created for your people. Think very hard about that."

"Why do I believe you're thinking more about what the truth would do to you JP? I wonder if you were ever honest with me. Please get out!"

Chapter 44

1977—Manhattan

Newport Naval station is located in Newport, Rhode Island. One of the base's many responsibilities was the mustering out of those sailors that served their country and were ready to leave the service. With his FBI contacts it took all of twenty minutes for Lou to track Lombardo down. A phone call to the base verified that he was in the process of retiring from the service. After contacting Lombardo by phone, a meeting was arranged.

"Pete Lombardo?" Iozzino asked.

"You're talkin' to him. What can I do for you?"

"My name is Agent Iozzino, and this is Lieutenant Mongelli. I was wondering if we could ask you some questions?"

"About the killing of my old compadres, I guess. I was just heading over to the mess hall for coffee. Please join me. This is my last week, you know. Twenty years and out."

"Congratulations", Mongelli offered. "We'll gladly join you."

Pete Lombardo was a rugged looking individual, his sharp angular features shaped from all those years in the sun. His hair was black with flecks of grey and cut short to military standards. His nose was slightly hooked. The creases in his uniform looked sharp enough to cut wood. The three stripes identifying his E-5 rank stood out against the white uniform. They entered the mess hall, poured some coffees, and made their way to a table.

"How can I help you guys?"

"Do we call you Pete or Satch?" Mongelli opened the conversation.

With a smile on his face, he answered. "No one has called me Satch since the old neighborhood. I prefer Pete."

"I want to go back to 1957, Pete. Back to the night of the brawl between the Berettas and the Kings."

"Is this going to be a problem for me, guys? Am I going to get in trouble, or cause trouble in any way?"

"No, it's not a problem. We're trying to determine if there is a link between what happened that night and the killings. Getting a perspective of what played out that night may help us. We're talking to the remaining Berettas, hoping that something one of you says may give us a lead."

Satch fired up a Camel blew a couple of rings and began to talk:

"I remember that night vividly. It was damp and there was a slight fog. The humidity clung to you like a wet paste. That night was a long time coming. The fuse on that bomb was started years earlier, when the Edenwald Projects were constructed.

"There were always skirmishes with the black guys. A lot of taunting went on between the groups, fistfights, girls on both sides harassed; but it was kept in check by the mob and the older guys who hung out on the Avenue. It was an uneasy relationship, but it seemed to work. That is until those two assholes brutalized that black chick, and to add insult to injury, JP decides to get the hots for Washington's cousin. That didn't go over too well with the blacks or the whites.

"JP had a plan worked out to meet these fuckers head on. We knew they would be traveling from Harlem using the Lex. We knew there wouldn't be too many coming by car. They didn't know the Avenue that well and there would be too many of them. We figured they would get up to 225th Street somewhere around 8:30 or 9:00pm.

"Johnny would send two of the Beretta Debs down to Gun Hill Road and 210th Street Station. That was a little more than a mile from the boys waiting at 225th Street. The station located between 210th and 225th was the 219th Street Station.

"We waited for them on the platform at 219th. I was parked near the pay phone at the station. When the phone rang, I picked up and took the call. It was one of the Debs letting us know the Harlem boys were on the 8:30 express. We had broken the lights on the platform when we got there, so it would be hard to see us in the twilight. We know where the doors would open so we covered each door with two or three guys.

The Harlem boys were caught by surprise when the doors opened. We rushed them, swinging bats and clubs as they tried to exit the train. Some went down; others panicked and pushed past us onto the platform. The conductor must have seen the fighting and attempted to close the doors. After three or four tries the doors closed and the train left the station.

"Six or eight blacks were trapped on the platform facing at least twelve of us. To escape, they jumped to the tracks and crossed to the downtown side. They made their way to the catwalk and started running. Their mistake was they were running towards 225th street. Five or six of our guys followed them and chased them up the catwalk. The rest of us headed down the stairs and took off towards 225th and the Avenue.

"We heard the rumble of the downtown Lexington Avenue Express. It was the 8:45, a through train that did not stop at any of the local stations. We could tell it was really moving. Everything shakes when it comes through. We weren't too concerned about our guys on the catwalk. We used to walk those catwalks for fun.

"That's when we heard the air brakes engage, but it wasn't just the normal breaking action. We heard the emergency hydraulics engage. That god-awful screeching of the brakes and the locked wheels skidding along the tracks told us that something was terribly wrong; nothing was going to stop seven cars weighing twenty-five tons. We were at 224th street, a block away from the station . . . ."

Pete began to sob, tears streaking down his face. "I see it every night in my dreams. At first it sounded like rain, but it was blood. And then pieces of bodies fell through the tracks, hitting the ground below."

He stopped speaking for a few minutes, taking deep breaths as if he couldn't swallow. After a couple of moments he continued.

"People were running every which way. Apparently, whatever fighting that was going on stopped. No one knew what was happening. Guys just disappeared. Because they didn't know what was happening, they all wanted to get as far away as they could from the horror. The street fighting broke up before the police arrived. I went home.

"Two days later I took a trip down to the church to talk to Father Martin. I needed to talk to someone who was not a relative or a friend. As I entered the church, I spied that Reinford broad coming out of the confessional. I wondered what in hell she was doing there, and why the confessional?

"I called JP and told him I had seen her. He told me not to sweat it. The following day I left for the Navy. I never looked back."

"Can you remember who it was that crossed the tracks to go after the colored guys?" Iozzino asked.

"I remember Geno Contelmo and Mike Scarpetta went after them. I'm not sure about the others."

"I think the noose is tightening, Billy," Iozzino considered, as they got into the cruiser.

"I think it's time to talk to the other side, Lou. Let's find Louis Washington."

"Shouldn't be hard. Another gangbanger making it. He got about two dozen Domino's Pizza shops."

"What a great country!"

Chapter 45

1977—The Bronx

Louis Washington carried himself well. The light tan three-button suit seemed to be made for him. Obviously, it was custom tailored. The dark brown shirt and tan striped tie matched well, as did his pointed oxford colored shoes.

Mongelli and Iozzino sat in the lieutenant's workplace watching Washington through the office window as he asked the desk sergeant for directions to Mongelli's cubicle.

"Tell me again, Lou, why he wanted to meet us here in the station rather than us going to him?"

"He said something about having to pick up his mother."

"His mother still lives in this shithole?"

"Ask him yourself. Here he comes."

"If memory serves me right you must be Mongelli," Washington said as he shook hands with the lieutenant. He turned to Lou. "And you are?"

"Special Agent Iozzino. Glad to meet you", he said as he gave Washington his hand.

"Please have a seat, Mr. Washington. Before we get to the business at hand, please tell us why you wished to meet here rather than your office in Manhattan?"

"Believe it or not, my mother still lives here in this garbage pail. Her memories and her friends are here. However, my new house is almost complete in Hampton Bays on Long Island. Even if I have to use force, I will be moving her out there."

"Congratulations on your success in the pizza business," Lou commented.

"When my father and cousin were murdered, we had little income. I was working in a pizza place at the time and was good at what I did. I actually enjoyed working there and became a fairly good cook and pizza maker.

"Before my Uncle, Peter and Tanya left America for France, my uncle left instructions with his stateside attorney to buy the pizza parlor with Tanya's money. The attorney bought it in my name, and handed it over to me. They also paid someone to help me get started in the business. One of the first challenges I was handed was a six month program in speech elocution. I opened up my second store in Harlem at the ripe old age of nineteen. Of course I was backed by my cousin's lawyers, and they continued to run interference for me

"The second store was a gold mine. I realized that pizza parlors in black neighborhoods were almost nonexistent. Out of my two dozen stores, you'll find that most are in black areas.

"Now that I've brought you up to date on my life, please tell me what you want to talk about, Lieutenant."

"I want to talk to you about that night in 1957."

"The night my father and cousin were killed. Why?"

"I'm sure you're aware of the recent deaths of a few old gangbangers from the Avenue. What they had in common was their connection to the now defunct Italian Berettas. Also, as Berettas, they were all present that night for the showdown with the Kings; a showdown that culminated with the horrible deaths of your father and cousin."

"You're really going to take a closer look at that so-called accident, and you think my reliving that day will help?"

"It can't hurt, Louis."

Washington lit a cigarette and leaned back.

"I remember the heat and humidity. It was 85 degrees at 8:30 in the morning. It was overcast and misty. We were going to get some rain before the day was out. It was just a shitty day. The smell from car and bus exhausts could choke a fuckin' horse.

"We were ready for the showdown. The plan was to have the Harlem contingent of the Kings take the 7:40 Lex to 219th Street. We figured on at least fifteen guys, which included several of the Dragons.

Half would get off at 219^{th,} and the remainder would continue on to 225th Street. Our crew from Edenwald would make our way west towards the Avenue. We thought we might be able to catch the whites by surprise.

"Our goal was to find Danny and Tony. We believed they would be down at the poolroom hiding or being protected by whitey. We were going to rush the poolroom while the Berettas were busy with the guys that got off the Lex at 219th, off them two mothafuckers and get out.

"We had no idea the Berettas were waiting on the 219th Street platform, hidden in the shadows waiting to meet the express when it pulled into the station.

"However, I was preoccupied with a different issue. Before we started our trek to the Avenue, I called the house. My mom informed me that my dad and Alicia were on their way to the Avenue to catch the 8:30 express from 225th. He was taking Alicia home. He had no idea of the pending brawl.

"It scared the hell out of me, and all I could think of was getting them out of harm's way. We were half a block from the Avenue, when I saw Claude across the lot behind the school. He let out a scream and cut across the back of the school. What he saw was JP and my cousin Tanya gesturing to one another. It appeared to me they were having an argument.

"I figured Claude could take care of himself; I had to get down to the station and find my father and cousin. I knew Claude was armed and if he put a cap in JP, so be it. We were almost to the Avenue when I thought I heard a shot. I figured Claude took care of JP.

"We turned the corner on 225th street onto the Avenue. They were waiting for us. To get up to the station platform I had to go through them. I just kept swinging the bat I was carrying, making my way to the stairs. I could hear the guys that got off at 219th. They were running up the Avenue under the train tracks, being chased. I thought it couldn't get any worse. I could hear the Lex approaching the station, but there was something wrong. It wasn't slowing down.

"All I could think about was my father and cousin. Were they still on the platform above? I didn't know what to do, and then it happened. *I realized what was wrong.* It was a southbound through express.

"It wasn't supposed to stop. But one moment it was traveling all out, the station platform rattling as it entered the platform; then the hydraulic brakes moaned; the wheels locked as the emergency brakes engaged. The noise produced from the skidding wheels and the air from the hydraulic emergency system drowned out all sound. It didn't slow down a bit—seven cars weighing 300,000 pounds each skidded through that station doing 40 miles an hour.

"I know the same thought went through all our minds; *someone died*. We stood there; black and white, staring up at the elevated tracks anticipating the worst; and the worst happened. Blood and body parts fell from the tracks. People were screaming and running. We couldn't move, and we were wet with blood and small pieces of body parts. Clarence Jackson was standing next to me staring at his arm. A piece of flesh attached itself to his shirt. He looked at me, tears in his eyes. The piece of flesh was brown; the victim was a black.

"I started running for the stairs leading up to the train platform. The Berettas had the stairways blocked. They wouldn't let me pass. Clarence and some of the guys pulled me back. We could hear the sirens from the fire trucks coming down the Avenue

"Clarence kept yelling at me to move my ass. They dragged me away. I still don't remember how we got back to Edenwald. There was no cousin or father waiting at the apartment. I knew in my heart what was left of them was littering the Avenue. I kept thinking the fire trucks were there to wash the blood and gore into the sewers. They were going to wash what was left of them into the fuckin' sewers!

"Whatever remains were found were buried two days later; in one box, in one grave, covered by one stone. It was ruled an accident. The *Daily News* carried a small article on page five. The train engineer told the authorities he thought there were several people on the platform near my father, but he wasn't sure. He also said it seemed as if the man was trying to grab the girl for balance, pulling her on to the track as he fell. They never found anyone who witnessed the incident.

"A few days after the incident, Quincy Adams, leader of the Harlem Kings called the house. Up to that point I hadn't had any contact with any of the guys. My mother and I just wanted to be left alone with our grief.

"Quincy passed on his condolences and said he felt terrible. He said they shouldn't have crossed over to the catwalk. They should have held their ground on the 219th Street platform. I asked him what in hell he was talking about. He must have realized I had been out of touch, with all the confusion occurring that night.

"What Quincy told me next made me sick."

* * *

"*They were waiting for us, Louis. When the train doors opened, whitey was waiting on the platform. They came at us as we were exiting. Some of us were on the platform, and many of us were in the train. The doors closed as we were trying to exit the cars. Not all of us were able to exit.*

"*The train left the station with most of our boys still aboard. We were outnumbered on the platform, and we panicked. We jumped to the tracks, and crossed over to the catwalk on the downtown side. We headed for the 225th Street platform, figuring on meetin' up with you guys. We realized they had crossed over and were coming after us. We made it to the 225th Street platform and made our way up the stairs leading from the catwalk to the platform.*

"*We saw the old man and the kid huddled near the edge of the platform, away from the stairs. We ignored them and pushed our way past them, trying to get away from the guys chasing us. We didn't know there was only a few chasing us. If we did, we would have turned on them.*

"*It was then we realized the noise and the ground shaking. It was the through express coming into the station. I turned to see how far whitey was behind us. They were climbing onto the platform. I saw one of them use the baseball bat he was carrying to push the old man. The man started to fall backwards, but he wasn't holding on to the child. It looked as if she was trying to keep him from falling. She wouldn't let go. They never had a chance.*

"*We knew the shit was goin' to hit the fan so we scattered. Didn't know until the next day it was your father and cousin.*"

* * *

Louis's hand shook as he lit another cigarette. The tears were flowing freely as he tried to regain his composure.

Mongelli asked softly. "You never found out which of the white guys pushed your father, and of course no one would come forward to talk to the authorities."

"There were no authorities, Lieutenant, and of course no one would come forward! It only took the police one day to rule it an accident and close it out. If you're dead guys are the boys who were on that platform, and their deaths are related to what happened, then good riddance. Someone is doing what I should have done many years ago."

Lou nodded. "You sure as hell had reason, Louis."

Louis lit another cigarette from the first. "If I knew who it was that did this do you think I would have waited twenty years to get revenge, Agent Iozzino? I don't have any more hate left in me."

Mongelli spoke. "I have another question for you, Louis. When Claude Brown left the group that night to go after JP and Tanya, was he sure it was them?"

"It was fairly dark as I remember, Lieutenant. Dark enough where I had a tough time identifying anyone, but I'm fairly sure it was them, judging by Claude's reaction. Claude would be able to spot Tanya if she were on the moon. He worshipped her. The idea that she was with that piece of shit Pascalli, was driving him crazy. He recognized her."

"And Pascalli? Was it him?"

"That I can't answer. I don't doubt that Claude believed it was him."

Iozzino said: "Then one of them killed Claude."

"If you say so, Agent."

After Washington left the office Lou poured two cups of coffee, handing one to Mongelli. They sipped their drinks slowly, not speaking for a few moments. Finally Lou spoke. "Whoever was responsible for killing Claude Brown would walk in a heartbeat. Any ambulance chasing lawyer would have them out, pleading self defense. They probably would get a medal for saving your life."

"You're right, Lou, but he died hard, and I can't see her doing him. However, she just might be covering for JP. I think I'll visit her and press a little. If she knows no charges would be filed, she might talk to me. I need to bring closure to that incident."

"I understand and agree, Bill. Let's change the subject and discuss the death of Washington's father and the cousin."

"When you visited Contelmo's widow, she described him as being a 'miserable tortured human being who paid for his sins.' It's true that witnessing the death of those two people would give anyone nightmares for life. But did the words she used to describe his state seem more extreme than the words describing Satch's demeanor or for that matter any of the other gang members?"

"When Satch told us that one of the guys who crossed the tracks was Contelmo, I had the same thoughts."

"Bill, I think I'm going to pay Mrs. Contelmo another visit. We'll meet back here, go to dinner, and compare notes."

Chapter 46

1977—The Bronx

"I appreciate your taking the time to see me, Mrs. Contelmo. I just have a few questions."

"Please, come in, Agent."

The smell of alcohol permeated the air. Although it was almost noon, she was still in her bathrobe, her hair disheveled. Her eyes were bloodshot, and she had a haggard look about her.

He walked behind her, following her into the living room. She walked over to the small bar set against the wall and retrieved her drink. "Care to join me in a drink, Agent?"

"No, thank you"

"Then please have a seat and ask your questions."

She took a seat on the couch and placed her drink on the glass coffee table. Iozzino sat across from her in one of the two stuffed chairs facing the couch.

"You're going through a tough period, Mrs. Contelmo. The loss of a loved one is terribly traumatic. I promise I won't take up too much of your time."

"For all I care, he can rot in hell. All of them can rot in hell!"

"By 'all of them', are you referring to the other victims who were slain?"

Tears were streaming down her face. She started sobbing, taking deep breaths. She placed her hands over her face and started rocking. Iozzino sat quietly, waiting for her to stop. After a few moments she composed herself and downed her drink. They sat quietly for a minute longer. Finally she rose from the couch.

"I'll be right back." She went into the bedroom and a few moments later came out carrying a piece of notepaper. She stopped by the bar, poured herself another drink, and returned to the couch. She handed the typewritten sheet to Iozzino.

"I can't live with this anymore. This is a copy of a letter I wrote to Tanya Reinhart. Please read this, ask your questions, and go."

I'm writing this because I can't stand living with the horror anymore. I have to make you understand the nightmare that has tortured me these last few months.

"*Your sister and uncle were killed that night twenty years ago. It was not an accident. The black boys panicked.*

"*They were trapped on the platform on 219th Street. They crossed the tracks to the southbound catwalk and made their way north toward the 225th Street platform. Four Berettas went after them, knowing the blacks would be caught between stations.*

"*The white guys, smelling blood, followed them to the 225th Street platform. They would trap them on the station platform. Chasing the black boys on to the platform, the Berettas saw the old negro guy and the kid. The problem was, all they saw was a black.*

"*They were oblivious to the Lexington Express racing through the station. All they saw was the enemy.*

"*One of the Berettas drove his bat into the chest of the black man, pushing him back. As he started to fall to the tracks, your sister tried to grab him. He struggled to release the girl's hold on him. She wouldn't let go. Both went off the platform into the path of the train. It was no accident. I know this because one of those bastards was my husband. He told me this a few months ago. He couldn't live with his nightmares after all those years.*

"*The four men who perpetrated this horror were Joe Rustico, Mike Scarpetta, Geno Contelmo and Marco Napolitano.*

"*After the incident, my husband brought it up to JP. He felt he needed to talk to someone about the episode. JP told him to drop it and not mention it to anyone, for Geno could be charged with conspiracy to commit murder.*

"*I'm writing this because I want you to understand how your loved ones died. I can't allow this to remain on my conscience any longer. It was no accident*".

"You didn't sign it."

"I was too ashamed to tell her my name. I also did not write a return address."

"Where did you send the letter?"

"I mailed it to Tanya Reinford's office in Manhattan. For her eyes only."

"Why didn't you give the letter to the police?"

"I wanted nothing more to do with that horrible night. Besides, knowing the police, they couldn't care less about an incident that happened twenty years ago to a couple of blacks. I did what I thought was right. How was I to know how she would react?"

"How did you think she reacted?"

"Obviously she had those bastards murdered. With her money she could buy a dozen assassins."

Lou raised himself off the chair. "I'm taking this copy of the letter with me. It's possible that this letter triggered the deaths of four men. It's also possible you were the catalyst in causing their deaths."

He left her sitting on the couch wallowing in her pitiful world and walked out the door.

Chapter 47

1977—Manhattan

"Lieutenant Mongelli, please come in. After receiving your phone call, I elected to ask our corporate lawyer, Michael Drace, to join us. Do you mind?"

"Not at all," Mongelli replied, shaking hands with Tanya and her lawyer. She showed the lieutenant into the office conference room.

The affluence of corporate America momentarily stopped Mongelli. The huge room held a forty-foot mahogany table surrounded by plush chairs. One twenty-five-foot wall was floor to ceiling glass, the whole of lower Manhattan caught in a panoramic view.

The opposite wall held dozens of framed prints containing photos of Tanya and her brother posing with famous African Americans, politicians from both political parties and celebrities from all over the world. Autographed pictures of Muhammad Ali, Frank Sinatra, Sammy Davis Jr., Catholic Cardinal Mindszenty, Al Pacino, Desmond Tutu, and dozens more adorned the wall. The bright red carpeting offset the subdued coloring of the remaining walls and ceiling.

The room was designed to reflect power and wealth, and lived up to its purpose. It was meant to intimidate.

"Please, have a seat. Can I get you something to drink? Perhaps a sandwich if you haven't eaten?"

"Coffee will be fine, Miss Reinford."

She pressed a small button on the console, situated at one end of the conference table. As beautiful as the surroundings were,

Mongelli thought, it was muted compared to Tanya's beauty. She wore her hair long, allowing it to tumble around her shoulders. Her face was oriental, with eyes that were slightly slanted, a trait from her Asian blood. Tanya's eyes took on a luminous look in the light. Her figure was flawless, the light grey pants-suit clinging to her body accentuating a perfect body. She was breathtaking.

"My brother will be joining us also, Lieutenant. Is that ok? I believe in safety in numbers." She smiled.

She's nervous, thought Mongelli. Before he could answer, the door opened, and her brother Peter walked in, a smile on his face. "Good afternoon, everyone." He walked over to his sister and pecked her on the cheek. Peter turned and greeted the family counselor.

"Good to see you, Michael"

"You, of course, are Lieutenant Mongelli." He walked over and shook the lieutenant's hand.

His facial features were the mirror image of his sister's. His hair was the same color as Tanya's; he wore it long into a ponytail. He was slightly taller than his sister but was very muscular. It was obvious he spent many hours at the gym.

Peter was strikingly handsome and made an imposing figure. His light grey Armani suit was custom tailored.

He wore a white shirt opened at the neck; a small gold cross offsetting his oriental coloring.

Michael Drace spoke, "Now that we are all here, Lieutenant, please enlighten us to the purpose of this visit. But before we begin, please assure us you will record nothing or take any notes. If this is not to your liking, then let us end this now. I have informed my client she has no responsibility to you or anyone else regarding events that occurred twenty years ago. It is against my advice that she meet with you. However, we are all very curious as to the nature of this meeting."

Mongelli turned to Tanya. "Thanks for taking the time to see me, Ms. Reinford. I assure you and your lawyer this is informal, and you are under no obligation to answer, or for that matter listen to what I have to say. However some of what I will cover may be disturbing. You may want to consider speaking to me in private."

Michael Drace spoke "This meeting is over now . . ."

Tanya interrupted, "Let him speak, Michael." She turned to Mongelli. "I have nothing to hide from Mr. Drace or my brother, Lieutenant, so please go on; and call me Tanya."

Mongelli hesitated for a moment "I want to go back to Thursday, July 25th 1957 . . ."

Peter interrupted. "That's enough, Lieutenant. How dare you resurrect the horror and pain of tha . . ."

Tanya turned to Peter, "Shut up, Peter, or leave." She turned to Mongelli, her eyes glistening. "Go on, Lieutenant."

She knows I know, Mongelli thought. *She's carried this burden all these years. She wants to let it out.*

Mongelli smirked and said in a sure, quiet tone,

"I'm sure you did your homework Tanya. You know who I am."

She smiled softly. "You still have a slight limp. I'm sorry."

He nodded his head, acknowledging her statement. "I was a rookie cop then, on foot patrol. I saw some boys heading up 226th Street towards Bronxwood Avenue. I followed them, thinking I could prevent some trouble.

"I saw some movement behind the school. Thinking it might be gang members, I headed towards the voices.

"When I got closer I saw three figures. I couldn't make out two of them due to the shadows, but the third one was very animated. And I as I approached I saw he was carrying a handgun. He was waving it around and yelling at the other people. He must have heard me approach.

"I told him to freeze and took my weapon out of my holster. My mistake. I should have had it drawn and in my hand. By the time I drew my weapon, he had turned and fired. I went down hitting my head and blacking out.

"When I was found several minutes later, the perp was lying on the ground dead from a knife wound, his gun by his side. The people he was arguing with were gone.

"The altercation was never looked into. Law Enforcement deduced that after he shot me, another gangbanger, white of course, killed the perp. As far as the law was concerned, good riddance. They never investigated, and until today the case was a dead file."

"What does this have to do with my client, Lieutenant?" asked Drace.

Staring at Mongelli, Tanya answered. "I was one of the other people at the scene, Michael."

Drace looked startled. "I think you said enough, Tanya. Lieutenant, this interview is over."

Tanya continued to stare at Mongelli. "No it's not, Michael."

Mongelli asked. "What happened, Tanya?"

Peter looked to his sister. "I think Tanya has been waiting a long time for this moment, Michael. Whatever she says or does, no harm can come to her."

Mongelli looked at Tanya. Tears were streaming down her face. She looked defeated, "Tanya?" Mongelli coaxed.

* * *

"I was staying at my cousin's house that night. My sister was also staying the night. I knew what was going down on the Avenue that evening. I felt it was better to stay in the apartment and leave the next day, after it was over.

"I went out to the store to buy a few groceries. When I returned my uncle and sister were gone. My aunt told me that Alicia was restless and wanted to get home to our dad. My uncle decided to take her home using the Lexington Avenue Express. It would be an adventure. He knew the train engineer would let her into the cab. It thrilled her, watching the stations and the lights fly by.

"I dropped the packages off and left the house. I had to get to the Avenue and intercept my uncle. The last thing I wanted was the two of them in the middle of a race war. I didn't have a car, and waiting for the bus was not an option. I hurried down 226th Street heading for the Avenue. I cut in back of the school heading for 225th Street when I heard my name.

"It was JP and Johnny Del in Johnny's car. JP got out of the car. He said something to Johnny Del, and Del took off. JP stopped me in back of the school. JP said, "Where the hell are you going?"

I told him my sister and uncle were heading for the Avenue to get the Lex. I had to stop them and get them off the Avenue."

"God damn it," he said. "It's too dangerous. Head back to your Aunt's house. I'll find them and get them back to you safely."

"I told him to let go of me but he refused".

"*You fuckin' whore!*" It was Claude Brown. He came out of nowhere. He screamed, "You an' this mothafuckin' honky think you got somethin' going. I'm goin' make sure you pigs don't touch each other ever again."

"He had a gun and was pointing it back and forth between JP and me. He was going to kill one or both of us. Then you showed up, Lieutenant. When you told him to freeze he turned on you.

"He turned on you and fired. You went to the ground hurt or dead. JP started to rush Claude. As Claude turned towards JP, I pulled my stiletto out of my boot and lashed out with it. I didn't even think about what I was doing. Claude hit the ground. He wasn't moving, the knife in his side.

"I stood there frozen. I think I blacked out. The next thing I realized, JP was placing me in Del's car. He told Del he would take care of things. I was in a daze.

"I don't remember the drive to the projects. Del was lightly shaking me. He was telling me, "Get upstairs, Tanya. Everything will be fine."

She was sobbing uncontrollably now, trying to catch her breath. Peter and Michael sat there looking shell-shocked. Mongelli got up and went to the credenza. He retrieved a box of tissues, handed Tanya a few, and placed the box in front of her.

"Self defense, Lieutenant. No prosecutor in the country would touch this." Drace was adamant.

Mongelli sat there and waited until Tanya composed herself.

"Are you up to answering a few more questions, Tanya?" She nodded, and Mongelli continued.

"In the days following the incident, what did you do?"

"I did nothing. I was in a daze following the death of Claude, my uncle, and my sister. I don't remember much. I don't remember much about the funerals. I was a zombie."

Peter spoke. "I can fill in, Lieutenant. We buried my uncle and sister a few days after they were killed. Two days later, my father, my sister, and I were on a plane to Paris, France. My father couldn't bear to stay in a racist, gun-crazy country any longer. He enrolled my sister and me in the Sorbonne.

"We never looked back. Eighteen years later, after my father passed away, we moved back here."

Mongelli nodded. "Thanks Peter." He stared at Tanya for a moment, lit a cigarette and then spoke.

"Mr. Drace is right Tanya. At the very most, if this went anywhere, which it won't, what you did, you did in self-defense. Now, I am going to ask you a question, and I want you to think very hard before you answer." She nodded.

"Please go through that moment when you stabbed Claude. Can you do that?"

"Lieutenant," Drace interjected. "Hasn't she had . . . ?"

She interrupted him. "After shooting you, he pointed the gun towards JP. He was going to shoot him. The knife came out of my boot. The next thing I remember, I was jamming it into his stomach. He went down and lay there."

"What happened to the knife?"

"As far as I know it was still in his side." The tears started to flow again as she relived the moment.

"I killed him, Lieutenant. I killed a friend, who was one of our own." She had her hands covering her face.

Mongelli gently removed her hands from her face. "Look at me, Tanya. You did not kill Claude."

She slowly removed her hands from her face. "What do you mean?"

"He was alive when you left him. The knife wound you inflicted did not kill him. It was the other one."

"The other one?"

"Yes, Tanya, the one that sliced his throat was fatal, not the wound to his side."

"But I didn't—*oh my dear God! JP!* All these years he made me think I killed Claude. He never told me the truth. That son of a bitch! My God! I had lunch with him the other day. He hit on me, wanted to resume our relationship. Things were better today, he said. We would be accepted."

Peter spoke. "Are you going arrest the miserable motherfucker?"

"It would be almost impossible. We have no direct proof; the only witness being Tanya. As Tanya said, it was self-defense. We have no weapon. His lawyers would tear us a new asshole. But at least you should be able to live with yourself now."

"God, thank you, Lieutenant, and to think I went to confession and admitted to killing Claude."

"Who was the priest, Tanya?

"Why it was Father Martin at Immaculate Conception on Gun Hill . . . . My God! Do you think his murder is related to this incident?"

Chapter 48

1977—The Bronx

Iozzino and Mongelli were parked in the Lieutenant's office. Lou had a putter in his hand and was putting balls across the carpeted floor, trying to get them to go into a water glass twenty feet away. He was not having much luck. Mongelli, his feet resting on his desk, was leaning back in his office chair with his eyes closed. He was not asleep. One week had passed since the meeting with Tanya Reinford.

"OK, Lou. You were on the phone all morning with your home office and now you seem a bit perky. What's up?"

"I believe we have a suspect in the ex-gangbanger murders. Wanna hear?"

"Sure. I can't wait."

"I don't believe Ms. Reinford received that letter. If she had, she would have handed it to you when she was going through her very emotional confession. Therefore, it was intercepted somewhere along the line by our perpetrator. If the letter went to Ms. Reinford 'for her eyes only' it would have ended up on her personal secretary's desk in a special stack of mail. Now, who would be in a position to not only see the envelope, but walk away with it?"

"No brainer. Peter Reinford."

"Right. Checking with his secretary, she confirmed

Mr. Reinford was in Tanya's office most of the week subsequent to Mrs. Contelmo's mailing of the letter. He was working on their new project, bringing TR Enterprises to France.

"I called the home office last night and asked them to somehow perform their magic. I gave them the dates and locations of the killings, and asked them to find out where Peter was on those days. They got back to me this morning. In every case, Peter was in position to easily perform the dirty deeds."

"How did they do that so quickly?"

Lou smiled. "My secretary in D.C. called his secretary and asked her where he was on those dates."

"Amazing! However, that evidence and fifty cents will get you on the Lex."

Lou putted. "Funny, but true. But I do buy him for the murders. We're sending agents to those locations, showing photos in the hope that someone will recognize him."

"Sounds like needle in a haystack, but worth a try."

Lou stopped putting and turned to Billy. "How are you going to handle the Claude Brown killing?"

"We have no case. Piscalli's lawyers would have a field day with us. The only witness, who, by the way saw nothing, was Tanya Reinford. Who's to say she didn't cut Brown's throat? It would be her word against the battery of lawyers defending JP. She admits to stabbing the guy. But, this bullet hole in my thigh makes it all moot. No matter how we twist it, it comes out self-defense."

"Too bad."

"Yeah, but I also like him for the priest's murder. Think about this, Lou. She knifes Claude. Believing she killed him, she goes to confession. Satch Lombardo sees Tanya enter the confessional and also sees her leaving.

"He thinks it was odd behavior so soon after all the tragedy. He calls JP and informs him he saw her.

"JP knows why she went to confession, but growing up a Catholic, he knows the priest cannot divulge what is said in the confessional."

Mongelli moved closer to Lou and continued. "In the priest's mind, Tanya is the killer. As far as JP is concerned, it's no sweat. But twenty years later, it is noted in the *Daily News* that Claude Brown's death was caused by a slit throat. The priest reads it, and JP reads it.

"The question becomes: Is the confession false? If so, is the priest still obligated to honor what was heard in the confessional, or can he share it? At the very least, can he share it with Tanya Reinford?

"JP has visions of being one of the most powerful and wealthiest people in America. Even if he would have no problem defending

himself, his reputation would suffer on several levels—from being a racist, to being a suspected killer. He couldn't let that happen."

Lou countered. "But he still had Tanya to contend with."

"I believe his ego would make him feel he could win her over and control her. But, you know what, Lou? I am going to make his world fall apart. He'll wish he never met Tanya Reinford. I am going to use her to bring him down."

"What about Johnny Del's roll in this?"

"I don't believe he knows anything about JP's involvement in the murder of the priest or the killing of Claude Brown. I'm not sure if he knows about the train incident. If he does, he's keeping his distance."

Chapter 49

The Bronx—1957

The rain cascaded through the openings in the tracks, running down the girders, falling to the street in large drops. It wasn't raining hard enough to wash away the filth that hugged the curb. The detritus discarded from the day's humanity pushed against it, refusing to release itself to the sewers that lined the streets.

The Avenue was empty and quiet. Several cars were lined up along the curb. There were no double-parkers. Following each shrill announcement of a Lexington Avenue Express entering the station, there came an exodus of people making their way quickly home to the safety of their apartments.

The neighborhood's violent events of the previous week; a cop shot, a black gangbanger dead, a tragic accident where an old black man and a child fell under the Lexington Avenue Express, and some store windows broken did not shake up the city's brass as much as the incident four days prior.

It was a different story then when Tony Chicarella and Danny Marconi, two white teenagers, were discovered shot to death. The car they were found in belonged to one of the deceased and was parked on the Avenue between 224th and 225th Streets. The bodies were placed in a sitting position. Both suffered multiple gunshot wounds to the head, a double tap; the trademark of a gang related assassination. The Mayor and Police Commissioner vowed to crack down on the criminal element in the Bronx, the particularly mob's presence on the Avenue. They added pressure to the street cops to keep things under control and put an even more dramatic halt to Anastasia's business.

Now, it seemed that everything was almost back to normal, except for the lack of people on the streets. Anyone loitering on the sidewalk in front of the stores, who looked twenty-one or younger, received a nightstick across the knees and was told to move on.

JP observed this from the Park Hill bar, staring out the window, holding a scotch and soda. He was oblivious to the cars pulling up and parking outside the Park Hill.

Due to the crackdown on double-parking, spaces for shoppers to park were at a premium. All the parallel parking spaces were taken up by the young gangbangers. Along the curbside, every space between 225th Street and 224th was occupied by a car belonging to one of the gang members. Present was Johnny Del's '50 Ford convertible, Tony's black and yellow Buick Roadmaster, Grazio's '55 convertible Chevy Impala. One by one they parked and made their way into the Park Hill. There wasn't much talking. They sat and sipped on their drinks.

Sally G entered the bar, ordered a drink, and walked over to JP.

"Gimmie a smoke."

JP handed him the pack of Camels. Sally G lit up and leaned on the window facing JP. "Notice somethin' out there, JP?"

"I notice the absence of life out there; so one must conclude the drug and numbers money probably ain't comin' in. Probably will be that way for a time."

Sally was bitter, the anger emanating from him.

"You guys really fucked up. Between you fuckin' that black bitch, nuzzlin' up to her; and your two boys playing ping pong with Washington's sister, you asswipes really put the screws to us. Anastasia is really pissed. There's no money comin' in, and the people he answers to blame him."

"I would say rightfully fuckin' so, Sally. Sure, it didn't help things that a black chick was raped and beaten; didn't help that I was fuckin' with a black broad. It didn't help that a black gangbanger is dead and a cop wounded. A guinea cop and a black. Those Irish fuckers in the 47th couldn't care less, but Anastasia, our Lord High Executioner, brought heat to the Avenue by capping Chicarella and Marcone.

"Those Mick bastard cops could have happily lived with the guinea hoods capping those two white asswipes; but instead of dumping them in the Jersey marshes, your boss, Mr. Anastasia, decided to put them on display for all to see in their car parked on the Avenue.

"By sending us a message to cool things with the blacks, he also sent a message to the law that he could get away with anything. That he was the man! And there wasn't anything they could do about it! Well, Mr. Hot Shot unleashed a fucking tiger when he did that. The Avenue will never be the same. I'll bet you a buck that Mr. Albert Anastasia will not be around this time next year."

Sally G was furious. "Listen to me, you punk motherfucker. I'll forget you said that. If it gets back to him that you're bad mouthin' him, you'll end up with a double tap behind the ear also. Anyway, what the fuck you goin' do for money without us around?"

"You give us chicken wings, Sally. Nickels and dimes you send our way for stealing and scamming for the mob. In a few weeks, at least five of us will be gone. Satch, Frankie, Little Tom, Del and I are all headed for the Armed Forces. Thank God!"

"Fuck you want to do that? You can't live that life man. You be crying in your sleep a week after you get wherever the hell you're going."

"Sally, I could be stationed in East Bumfuck, Alabama. It would still be a thousand times better than hangin' out in this armpit. If I never see the Avenue again it will be too soon."

"You're full of shit, man. I'll leave ya' to your thoughts, JP. I gotta go get me another drink."

JP lit another cigarette from the first and stared out at the rain.

He couldn't get her out of his mind. Tanya—she was gone. Three days after burying the remains of her uncle and sister, they left for France; Tanya, her brother, and their father. She never said goodbye, or even left word that she was leaving.

JP mused over what had happened *I cut that bastard Claude's throat for her. He would have never let it rest. Claude would have told the world she stabbed him and I helped her. The black gangbangers would find us and destroy us both. Worse, Claude would have recovered from his knife wound, done his prison time for shooting that cop, and then come after us. We would have always been looking over our shoulders waiting for him. She refuses to see me or get in touch; let her live with the belief she killed him. She deserves it.*

Chapter 50

1977—Manhattan

"Thanks for seeing us on such short notice."

Mongelli shook Tanya's hand. "I'm glad your brother could join us as well as your attorney Mr. Drace."

Peter spoke, "I hope this is important. As you can see, my sister is really not up to speaking to anyone at this time."

Tanya looked at Peter. The stress was showing in her eyes. "I can speak for myself, Peter."

It was obvious to the law officers that Tanya Reinford was going through her own private hell. She looked drawn and disheveled. She wore no makeup. Her eyes were red rimmed with dark circles and glistening with tears.

"Please say what you have to and leave me in peace."

She stared into Mongelli's eyes. With all her grief, her gaze was dark and hard. A tremendous amount of anger radiated off of her.

I'm sure glad that anger isn't directed at me, Mongelli thought, *but it's nothing compared to what she is going to feel when I'm through.*

"Let me begin by telling you that what I'm about to tell you is not pleasant and will bring you more hurt." "Then perhaps you should discuss it with Peter and me first, apart from Ms. Reinford's presence, and then we can be the judge of when to tell her this news," their lawyer Michael Drace offered.

"Like hell, he will, Michael. Go on, Lieutenant. It's going to be tough to make me feel any worse than I do now," Tanya said.

Mongelli continued, "We believe there may be a link between your confession to Father Martin and his murder. We think that link may lead us to Mr. Piscalli. If the truth came out regarding the death of Claude Brown, it could seriously hurt JP financially and politically.

"He wasn't sure if the priest would be in a position to recant on his vow of silence; his logic being the confession was not true. We believe he didn't want the priest getting back to you with the truth."

She sat there stunned. The room was quiet for a moment.

Finally Tanya spoke. "So I could be indirectly responsible for another death, Lieutenant?" She buried her face in her hands taking deep breaths.

"Are you going to arrest him?" Peter offered.

"We don't have enough evidence," Mongelli countered.

"We may have a couple of people who might have seen him at the church the day of the murder. It's a slim lead, but we're following up. What we have now is nothing but conjecture. We will continue to follow up on the leads we have. We thought you should be aware of our suspicions."

They sat for a moment in silence. She removed her hands from her face and stared intently at Iozzino, who had been suspiciously quiet.

"There's something else isn't there, Agent Iozzino?"

He hesitated for a moment before he spoke. In that moment he decided to speak to Peter without her being in the room. He perceived that Tanya looked almost catatonic. He knew she never received the letter. To bring the issue up after the blows that were just dealt her would be too much for her to handle at this time. There was no doubt she would arrive at the same conclusion as the detectives. In any case she would be told, but now she needed time to recover.

"We would like to speak with your brother regarding another matter. It's not necessary for you to be here."

Tanya spoke forcefully "If I want to stay?"

Peter answered "It's quite alright, Tanya. I have Michael to protect any interests of ours that may be compromised."

Michael turned to Iozzino "Is this necessary, Detectives?"

Iozzino replied "I'm afraid it is, sir."

Tanya rose from her chair. "I'm going home, Peter. Please call me later." She walked out of the conference room without looking back.

*   *   *

"Please go ahead, Agent Iozzino, we're listening," Peter spoke.

Lou took Gracie Contelmo's letter out of his pocket and opened it. He handed it to Peter. The lieutenant, watching Peter, realized the stoic look on Peter's face meant that he knew exactly what was in the letter. Peter looked at the letter and handed it to Michael.

"Where did this come from?" Peter asked. "This is horrible. Has my sister seen this? This confirms everything we believed. Our sister and uncle were killed. Their deaths were no accident."

The lawyer spoke. "This opens up a whole new component regarding the deaths of their sister and uncle if it wasn't an accident and they were murdered. Why wasn't this made public?"

Iozzino looked him in the eye "Maybe Peter might answer that, sir."

Peter spoke "What the hell are you talking about?"

Iozzino replied "A few weeks ago, the original of this letter was mailed to Ms. Reinford, here in her office. It is obvious she never received it. Somewhere along the route, it was intercepted, probably here. Ms. Reinford's mail comes into the office and is sorted by her secretary, then placed in order of importance.

"Someone went through Ms. Reinford's mail, saw the letter without a return address, was curious, and lifted it. According to her Tanya's secretary, Peter, you usually sorted through the mail for anything of importance. Her secretary Suzie was fairly certain you took the envelope with the letter. I believe Tanya has no idea this letter exists, and I believe that you knew exactly what was in the copy I just handed to you."

Michael was visibly upset. "This is terrible, and I understand the impact it would have on Ms. Reinford. I can understand Peter's reluctance to show his sister something so horrible."

Iozzino spoke to Michael but stared at Peter "The four men mentioned in the letter are dead. They were murdered. I believe they were revenge murders. The only person who knew who they were and would want revenge would be Tanya or Peter. Tanya knows nothing of this letter."

Michael got up to leave. "This meeting is over gentlemen. Let's go, Peter."

Peter rose and followed Michael, a tight smile on his face.

As they were leaving the room, Iozzino turned to Peter. "What are you going to tell your sister, Peter? You think she's not going to come to the same conclusion we did? You killed those men. She is going to know this."

Peter looked at Iozzino, the hate spilling from his eyes. "Fat chance you'll prove it. But you know what, Agent Iozzino? Who deserved to die more than those maggots?"

Michael grabbed Peter by the arm. "Shut up, Peter. I said this meeting is over. Goodbye gentlemen."

As they were leaving the office Iozzino stopped by Suzie's desk. "Can I use your copier please?" He asked

"Would you like me to do that for you, sir?"

"No, thank you. However, can you please get me a business envelope with Ms. Reinford's name typed as the recipient?"

"Of course."

Upon returning from the copier, Iozzino folded the copy of the letter and sealed it in the business envelope.

"Please see that Ms. Reinford gets this letter in tomorrow's delivery. It's important that you wait until tomorrow, and please hand it to her personally. Do not give it to anyone else."

"I'll hand it to her personally, sir."

As they were waiting for the elevator, Iozzino turned to Mongelli. "Please get that 'I don't want to know' look off your face. I just want to get this moving. It needs to be all out on the table."

"I don't want to know look?" Mongelli started to chuckle. "I believe in the coming days the recipient of all the built up hostilities, anger, and pain enveloping these people will be Mr.Pascalli."

"It couldn't happen to a better person."

Chapter 51

1957—October

JP was leaning against the plate glass window in the Park Hill along with an ashtray holding his cigarette, the smoke curling towards the ceiling. Although the temperature in the restaurant was comfortable, JP continued to wear his car coat. The wind, although muffled, could still be heard inside the bar whistling up the Avenue. The steel pillars supporting the elevated train structure and the stores lining the streets created a tunnel for the south wind. Detritus, in the form of old newspapers, dust, and discarded items of everyday use, was carried along with the wind.

The bite of winter was in the air. The door opened and Sally G entered the bar. He looked at JP and then ordered a drink. Drink in hand; he walked over to the window. He lit a cigarette and stared at the *Daily News* in JP's hands.

JP smiled. "You always get more in the Sunday edition. Just in case you haven't seen it, I gotta read you this page-three story." He opened the newspaper to page three and began to read.

"He Died In the Chair After All"

"Albert Anastasia, 'Lord High Executioner' of Murder Inc., was rudely dispatched from his throne yesterday when two gunmen walked into the Park Sheraton Hotel, pumped four bullets into him as he sat in a barber chair, and left him for dead. Thus did the

gangster who beat the chair five times wind up his career of crime."

JP chuckled. "Apparently, you have a vacancy in the top echelon, Sally."

Sally G answered, "There's never a vacancy, JP. Anastasia was a sadistic, sick prick. It was a long time coming."

JP retorted, "You think the Avenue helped bring him down?"

Sally G smiled at JP. "What the fuck do I know? All I know is that business has been terrible since those killings back in July. I have a feeling things will change with Genovese at the helm."

Sally G continued, "The Avenue is dead. As soon as there are more than a couple of guys hanging out, a cop shows up to chase them. It's hard to do business around here."

JP gave a sarcastic laugh. "It doesn't go over too big when the fuzz discovers a couple of teenagers parked on the Avenue with holes blown in them, regardless of who did it."

Sally G replied, "When Genovese takes over Michael Cappola will cover his back."

JP looked at Sally with surprise. "Cappola from 227th Street? I thought he was on the shit list. Something about him losing some money."

Sally G took a drag on his cigarette. "He made good on it, but he swears it was stolen. He's still one pissed off son of a bitch."

Sally G finished his drink. "I gotta split. See you around."

"Not for long. A couple of weeks, I'll be gone."

JP went back to staring out the window after Sally G left. A light rain began to fall. He heard the Lex pull into the station, its brakes groaning as the train was forced to stop. The weather was dismal. It seemed to fit his mood.

He was depressed but didn't know why. He kept fingering the medal Tanya had given him after having sex in the rear seat of his car. He missed her terribly. She didn't answer any of his letters, so he stopped trying to get in touch with her. He refused to believe she gave up on him. JP believed they belonged together, regardless of the racial issues. He knew he had twisted emotions. How could he hate blacks but love her? In his egocentric mind he believed she would come to him, that color would not be an issue.

If Claude Brown were allowed to live, he would have been a threat to JP and Tanya. In his selfish, egotistical mentality, JP believed he had to kill Claude, and making her think she killed Claude would drive her into his arms. He thought she would need him for support. It was too bad about her sister and uncle, but she couldn't put blame on him for their deaths. Shit happens.

The rain came down harder, the wind driving the rain into the window, giving off a staccato rhythm as it beat against the glass.

His mind drifted back to the summer. He thought of the trips the guys made to Jones Beach on Long Island and the barbeques at Glen Island in Westchester. But his thoughts always came back to Orchard Beach, to the day he watched her as she walked towards him. He knew at that moment he had to have her, to own her. She would be his.

The Avenue was quiet now. Strange, that there were no cars double-parked, even for a Sunday. But the boys are gone, JP reflected. Satch, Grazio and Little Tom, all in the service. Chicarella and Marconi dead and buried and rotting in hell for the tempest they unleashed. The Shack Boys are staying away, and you can't blame them.

Couple of weeks Del and I will be gone, nobody left. There will be no Avenue to come back to. Fuck it! If I don't hear another Lexington Avenue Express ever again, it will be too soon.

The door opened and Del came in shaking the rain off. "L-Let's get going, JP. We have t-to meet T-Terri and Annie in 15 minutes. After d-dinner we'll head over to Annie's apartment. It's a g-great night for some lovin."

"Yeah, let's get the fuck outta here. Thank God *Terri* will always love me."

175

Chapter 52

1977—Manhattan

The day after the detectives' visit, Tanya opened the letter. After reading it, she saw the short note written by Agent Iozzino.

Tanya, you may want to ask your brother about this letter or ask your secretary.

Suzy, her secretary, heard her swearing through the open door. Tanya called her, cancelling all appointments for the near future. She then instructed her to have the car ready to take her home.

Two days after the detectives' visit, Tanya came out of the seclusion of her apartment and proceeded to her office. She spoke to no one as she passed by her staff, entered her office, and closed the door. A short time later, she called her secretary to come into her office.

"First, please bring me some fresh coffee, Suzy. Have my brother join me in my office as soon as he comes in."

A few moments later Peter entered the room, sat in one of the plush chairs, and lit a cigarette.

"I'm glad your back, Sis. I was worried."

"I'll never forgive you for stealing that letter, Peter."

"I won't apologize for it, Sis. I thought I could save you some grief."

"Bullshit! I'm not a stupid person. Make sure you're here tomorrow. Now, I have a lot of catching up to do so I'd like to get to work."

After Peter left the room, Tanya buzzed Suzy. "Yes, Tanya?"

"Call our lawyer Michael Drace; I need to speak with him as soon as possible. Also, find Mr. Piscalli. Ask him if he can join me for dinner tomorrow night, eight o'clock at Forlini's. I'm sure he's familiar with the restaurant. Also, I read in this morning's paper that Sammy Davis Jr. is in town. He's appearing at the Copacabana this weekend. Find him and ask him to call me as soon as he can."

A few moments later Suzy was on the intercom.

"I have Mr. Davis on the line, Ms. Reinford."

"Tanya, my beautiful friend. Tell me you'll marry me, and I'll drop everything and rush over."

"Give me a chance to say hello first, Sammy. How are you?"

"Fine, especially after hearing your voice."

"Listen, I know you get together with your buddies for dinner when you're in town. I'd like to see you guys, but between your schedule and mine it's hard to connect."

"Join us for dinner, darlin'. The boys would go ga-ga over you."

"Well, I'm meeting someone for drinks tomorrow night at Forlini's. I know it's one of your favorite restaurants. Perhaps you'll be there?"

"Love that place. We'll make it a point to be there."

"Is Frank going to join you guys?"

"Don't tell me you got the hots for Mr. Sinatra. You're breaking my heart. Besides he's white! Of course he's going to join us."

"No, he's not my type. I know he likes to get together with some of the Italian guys who walk on the wild side, and I know he's good friends with Michael Cappola. He usually invites him out to have dinner with you guys, seeing he is married to Frank's cousin. Would he be joining you also?"

"Now you have me scared. You're up to no good. You are aware that it's rumored he is a captain in the Genovese family. Of course, it's nonsense. Chances are he will be joining us. He's a good friend, and you shouldn't believe everything you hear. I'm not even going to ask you why you're interested in Cappola, but I don't believe it's going to help your reputation."

"Fuck my reputation. See you tomorrow night at Forlini's."

* * *

The following morning Tanya, Peter, and Michael Drace met in Tanya's office. As soon as the coffee was poured, Tanya got to the crux of the meeting. Peter recognized the steel look in Tanya's eyes. She was all business.

"Peter, you are to leave before the end of the week for France. You are aware of our vested interest in TK enterprises. Eventually we hope to establish our world headquarters in that country. You are to take over as CEO of TK Enterprises, France, Ltd. You are to establish residence, and as soon as it's feasible, you will apply for French citizenship. You will carry dual citizenship. I will run operations here in the U.S."

"I suppose I don't have a choice, Sis. To tell you the truth, I like the idea."

"Michael, work out any foreseeable issues or problems. Starting today, any attempts by law enforcement of either country to communicate with Peter must go through you and me."

Drace nodded. "No problem, Tanya. Is there anything else I should know?""

"No, and if there are no questions, this meeting is over." She got up and headed for the door. As she was exiting, she turned to Peter. "Have a great trip, Peter, and you are not to come back to the States for any reason without checking with me first."

Chapter 53

1977—Manhattan

"Good Evening, Mr. Piscalli. It's a pleasure having you back."

"Is my table available? I know I haven't called, so I will understand if it's not available. Perhaps . . ."

"Ms. Tanya Reinford called. She made a reservation and asked to be seated at a specific table. She mentioned that you would be joining her. I hope it meets with your approval."

JP smiled, "Of course, Robert."

"We had to create a special setup to accommodate her request. We had refurbished that particular corner, so we tried to adjust to her request as best we could," the maitre d' responded.

"I'm sure it will be fine."

The table arrangement was a throwback to the night he and Tanya were on their first date. The tablecloth, the candles, the wine chilling off to the side, unopened. The memories of that night long ago flooded back. He fell in love that night, and he was sure she cared for him. He refused to believe the reality that he was responsible for the chasm between them. He realized he still loved her and had to win her over.

"Mr. Piscalli."

JP realized he was standing there, his mind caught up in the past. He realized that Robert was talking to him. "This is fine, Robert. Bring me a Glenlivet on the rocks, please." He sat, lit a cigarette, and wondered what the next few hours would bring him.

She entered the lounge ten minutes later. It seemed to JP that the noise level in the restaurant dropped significantly when she walked through the door. The cocktail dress she wore clung to her, slim straps holding it to her body. It was a backless creation, the straps the only means of support. She was wearing no bra. The deep cleavage of the dress exposed most of her breasts, and with her bare midriff, left little to the imagination. The garment started just above the knees, her beautiful legs accentuated by the three inch heels she wore. With the pale yellow of the dress complementing the light color of her skin, she was stunning.

As Robert was escorting Tanya to the table, she stopped several times to greet friends and business associates.

One of the waiters whispered in Robert's ear. Robert, in turn, turned to Tanya as she was saying goodbye to Paul Harvey, famed broadcaster.

"You give me your word, Tanya; you will give me an interview. Your life story will give me another chapter in my book, and you promised to tell me 'The rest of the story.'"

She smiled, "You have my word, Paul."

Robert whispered in Tanya's ear. "Sammy Davis is asking if you will join him and some friends for drinks."

Tanya looked to the entertainer's table and waved. She recognized several of the Rat Pack as they waved back.

"Tell Mr. Davis I will join him and his friends shortly, as soon as I take care of some business."

She took notice of Michael Cappola sitting across from Sinatra. She smiled.

JP rose to greet her as she made her way to the table.

"If I knew you were this popular, I would have asked you to select a less known restaurant, where we might have more privacy. You look absolutely beautiful." He moved to kiss her on the cheek; she ignored the gesture and sat.

"May I please have a cold Grey Goose martini straight-up with one olive brought over, Robert?"

"Certainly, Ms. Reinford."

"How are you, JP?"

"I'm fine, Tanya. I was hoping you had second thoughts after our last meeting. But obviously, by asking to meet me here, you have a different agenda. I get the feeling I was set up. Based on your entrance and your table hopping, not to mention the million dollar look, you were sending me a message."

"That is very astute of you, JP. Did you believe I would rush into your arms; that we would dash out of here, and we would fuck our brains out?"

"Something like that. Who are you kidding, Tanya? I know you have feelings for me. We had something great, and I don't believe the feeling has diminished that much over the years."

Chapter 54

1977—Manhattan

She showed no emotion as she spoke. "Let me tell you what I feel, JP. You are a murdering, treacherous, lying son of a bitch. You haven't got one ounce of decency in you. You murdered Claude Brown twenty years ago, and you led me to believe I killed him. You knew my sister and uncle were pushed off that platform by your scumbag friends. For twenty years you let us believe it was an accident; that it was my uncle's fault my sister died, when in fact she was trying to pull him back from the edge of the platform.

"You murdered Father Martin. You panicked and thought he would not have to keep his vows to honor my confession, that he would come to me, and then go to the police with the truth. You need to pay for that, JP."

The soft look shown by JP when greeting Tanya was replaced by a hard glint. His body tightened. He looked like a trapped rodent. She thought for a moment that he would reach across the table and smack her.

Then, just as suddenly, he relaxed. He lit a cigarette, sipped his scotch, and smiled. "That's very good, Tanya. Did you rehearse that little speech? Let's get realistic. The killing of Claude Brown was self-defense. A wounded cop, a black perp holding the weapon, cut down by a couple of people who feared for their lives. It could never go to court, could never be tried. If anything, we are heroes. He shot the cop and was going to shoot us.

"After you stabbed him and left, *Tanya,* I saw he was still alive and was raising his gun to shoot me. I defended myself. What happened

182

to the knife is beyond me. So let's forget that one. I didn't tell you I killed him because you and your family disappeared shortly after the killing."

"You could have gotten in touch."

"It would have changed nothing. Besides, I was pissed that you left without saying a word.

"As far as the incident with your sister and uncle, what would it have changed? No one would be able to prove they were pushed on purpose, and who knew what the truth was then?

"Of course, Contelmo's confession did point to the truth, but it was twenty years too late. Don't look so surprised that I know about the confession. Gracie Contelmo called me."

JP face was tight, daggers coming out of his eyes.

"Do you honestly believe I would have gone to the police after Geno Contelmo told me what actually happened? You believe I would turn in one of my own, just to give you some closure? Not a chance."

Tanya spat out the words. "You *bastard*! Just to protect some white-trash motherfucker, you let everyone believe my uncle took my sister to her death. You must have really loved me not to come to me!"

"Not an issue anymore, is it, Tanya? As far as the priest is concerned; I won't even go into that, as I haven't got the faintest idea what you're talking about.

"Speaking of killings, Tanya, who do you think killed my childhood friends? I'm sure you must have an idea."

"Whoever killed them did society a favor, JP. Unfortunately you weren't among them. But you're going to pay, JP. I can almost guarantee it."

"Tanya, you come in here, a beautiful vision; shake hands, say hello to the rich and famous, wave to your celebrity friends to show me how powerful you are.

Check the Fortune 500 darling. I could almost buy and sell you, and probably will in a few years. You're no threat to me, Tanya."

She smiled and stood. She took her drink and looked at him. "I would throw it in your face, but that would be tacky. As the Italians say, 'Salud.'" She finished the drink and walked away.

Chapter 55

Manhattan—1977

"Sammy, it's good to see you." Tanya kissed him on the cheek. Sammy Davis rose from his seat and gave Tanya a hug. "My God, you are a vision. You light up the table. Sit and I'll introduce you to my companions." A chair appeared, and Tanya was seated between Sammy and Frank. She had met most of the people surrounding Sammy and greeted them all by name, including the two she hadn't met but knew by reputation. Sammy introduced her to Michael Cappola and Sam Giancana, kingpins in the Mafia. Sinatra ordered a fresh martini for Tanya. He smiled at her. "Great to see you, Tanya. Hope you stay awhile so we can talk. I have a movie proposition for you."

"You have my attention, Frank. Let's talk later tonight and set a date for next week to discuss it," an excited Tanya replied.

A few minutes later, the group was complimenting Sammy on his new show and all gave a toast to its success.

"Tanya, I understand you're thinking of branching out to my field?" John Johnson, publisher of EBONY magazine, chided her.

"John, no magazine can compete with EBONY. I am toying with the idea of publishing a fashion magazine though. Obviously the main subject would be the world of fashion."

"When you decide, please get in touch. I can help."

"Absolutely."

Giancana was wrapped up in a conversation with the actress Lola Falana, while most of the others were discussing Sammy's next five days at the Copa.

Tanya caught Michael Cappola staring at her. When he caught her eye, he spoke, "You are truly a most beautiful woman, Miss Reinford. Your photo on the cover of *Business Week* brings out your beauty, but even that photo does not do you justice."

"Why thank you, Mr. Cappola. You know; I remember hearing your name in a conversation about twenty years ago. It sticks in my mind because of the circumstances. I think you will be interested."

He rose, took his chair and planted it next to Tanya

"Excuse me, gentlemen. This beautiful woman has an anecdote she wants to share with me.

"Call me Michael; may I call you Tanya? Now, tell me."

"Twenty years ago you lived in a tenement on 227th Street in the Bronx. In fact you lived on the third floor."

"Now you're fascinating me, Tanya."

"At the time you were in the banking business, and at certain times of the week you handled very large amounts of money."

The smile on Cappola's face disappeared. "Where are you going with this, Tanya?"

"Trust me; you won't regret it, Michael."

She continued, "One night in the summer of 1957, someone entered your apartment and stole three thousand dollars that didn't belong to you. I'm sure you suffered greatly, personally, and monetarily for that loss. I'm also sure you had to replace that money out of pocket, and that had to be a great hardship.

"The person who climbed the fire escape to your apartment and stole that money is sitting at the table I just left. His name is Johnny Piscalli."

"How do you know this, Tanya?"

"He told me about it, sitting in the backseat of his car. He was trying to get into my pants and thought it would impress me. It was right after I had given him a small gift."

"Were you impressed?"

"Not enough to let him get into my pants." *What the hell,* she thought; *just a little white lie.*

"Did he say how many others were with him?"

"He named two others, but they passed away not too long ago. They were killed."

Tanya was on a roll. "JP told me the job was easy. He said the word on the Avenue was that you were on Anastasia's shit list for awhile." *Did he say that? Can't hurt.*

"Let me tell you a little story, Tanya. Two days after I told Anastasia I was three thousand short, he had me on my knees with his piece pressed against my temple. He told me I had thirty seconds to tell him what I did with the money, or I was a dead man.

"I was twenty-three years old, Tanya. Genovese walked in and stopped him. He told Anastasia I would pay it back. I would work for Vito. I did shit work for a long time, Tanya. I prayed that nothing would happen to Genovese, because I knew Anastasia would put a cap in me in a heartbeat.

"This little story doesn't get beyond us, Tanya; you understand?"

"Of course, I understand, Michael."

"I have just two questions, Tanya. What did Piscalli do to make you hate him this much? And tell me again what you gave him when you were dancing in the back seat of his car?"

"I gave him a medal of Saint Jude in a moment of passion. Why I hate him is a story that spans twenty years, Michael. I'll tell you about it someday

"Sammy's giving me the high sign; I should spend some time with him and Frank. Nice meeting you, Michael"

"Tanya, we never spoke about this."

"Spoke about what, Michael?"

Epilogue

October—1977

"Hello Tanya. This is Johnny Del, returning your call."

"Johnny, I wonder if you can meet me for lunch today? I realize how busy you are now that you're filling in for JP, but if you can spare the time . . . ?"

"Of course I can. Why don't I meet you at Smith & Wollenskys Steakhouse in midtown? I'll have a table reserved for us; say about one p.m.?"

"It's my favorite new restaurant. Great, I'll see you at one."

"I'm looking forward to seeing you, Tanya."

Del placed the phone in its cradle and sat back. After a moment he used his keys to unlock the bottom right hand drawer of his desk. He removed the large manila envelope from the drawer and opened it. The knife slid out of the envelope and fell onto the desk. It was encased in a plastic bag. He picked up the bag and examined the knife, turning it over in his hands. After twenty years there was still some residue on the knife, remnants of dried blood. It's time to give the knife back to its owner. He sat there and stared at the weapon, memories of that fatal night swirling in his mind.

The intercom interrupted his thoughts. "Mr. Delgardo, just a reminder. You will be convening the Board in fifteen minutes."

"Thank you."

*   *   *

Mongelli and Iozzino were in the lieutenant's office in the usual positions. Mongelli was sitting with his feet resting on the desk and Iozzino was practicing his putting.

"What do you think happened to him, Lou? He just vanished from the face of the earth."

"He's either resting in the swamps of New Jersey, or he's sleeping with the fish out in Long Island Sound."

Mongelli was tapping the pencil he held in his hand against his forehead. "The only people who had that kind of grudge are the Reinfords; but somehow I can't see them for this killing."

Lou put one in the glass from fifteen feet and pumped his fist. "I don't think it was Peter. He knows we're on his ass for the gangbanger murders. My investigators placed him in Vegas at Hemingway's bistro with a hooker the night Joe Rustico was capped. We're closing in on him."

"You'll never get him, Lou. With his high-priced lawyers and the clout he has, he'll run you in circles forever."

"You're probably right, Billy, but we'll keep trying. No matter how badly those gangbangers needed to die, murder is murder. We'll keep digging."

Billy lit a cigarette. "We're pretty sure JP killed the priest. We found two very old Italian mommas who saw JP leave the church that day. They were there for their daily prayers. We just have to pinpoint the time."

"You're not going to find Piscalli, Billy. He's dead. With all their posturing, the Mayor, the Governor, and the business community are not bringing him back."

"Well, Lou, thank God I'm retiring."

*　　*　　*

Hanging up the phone, Tanya leaned back in her chair and momentarily closed her eyes. When she opened them, she was staring at the picture of her baby sister waving to the camera. Draped over the picture was a medal depicting Saint Jude, Patron Saint of Lost Causes. The medal was delivered to her several days ago in a plain envelope with no writing on it. It was delivered by a young boy with instructions that it was to be given to Tanya Reinford personally.

He received a five-dollar tip for his efforts. When she opened the envelope, the medal fell to the desk. She stared at it for a moment, then picked it up and draped it on the picture. For one brief moment she felt a touch of remorse; then it was gone. She smiled. My family thanks you, Michael Cappola, she whispered.

*　　*　　*

She wore a white trench coat that stopped several inches below the knee. Under the coat she wore a pale green miniskirt with a dark green turtleneck sweater.

The maitre d' couldn't believe one of the most popular, beautiful, and influential woman in America graced his restaurant. Heads turned and conversation died as he led her to Del's table. She sat and ordered a Gray Goose martini straight up. Johnny already had a Laphroaig single malt scotch sitting in front of him.

"Watching you walk into a room full of people cracks me up, Tanya. You are truly an incredible person."

She laughed easily. "To tell you the truth Del I get a kick out of it myself." The smile left her face.

"It's time for you to tell me what happened that night. I've heard it a dozen ways, but I haven't heard it from you."

"I figured you wanted some closure, Tanya, but there are no surprises." He paused and lit a cigarette.

"We were in my car. Supposedly checking to confirm our guys were ready. JP was agitated and showed it. I knew he didn't fear the upcoming fight.

"I asked him. 'What's up, JP? You're antsy as hell'. He told me to head up 225th Street, towards the projects.

"Earlier JP called your Aunt's house. He was told you weren't home. Your Aunt said you went looking for your sister and uncle; that you were probably headed for the Avenue."

Tanya nodded. "I remember it vividly."

"JP was in panic mode. I remember him saying 'I gotta find her, Del. Her uncle and sister were probably headed for the train station. She's gotta be on 225th Street or 226th.'

"I told JP, we have enough trouble without lookin' out for his girlfriend." He just said, 'Please drive, Del.'

"We saw you running down 225th Street towards the Avenue. You were right near the school. I pulled over to the curb and JP Jumped out of the car. I waited in the car, keeping an eye out for any of the Kings. He stopped you and pushed you towards the back of the school. You two were going at it. You went at him screaming, Tanya. *'Goddamn you, JP, let me be. My sister and Uncle are heading right into the middle of your little race war. I need to get to them.'*"

Del continued, "JP told you to get in the car. He said he would find them."

Del paused and lit a cigarette. "I heard the Kings yelling and screaming as they came down 226th Street. I saw Claude Brown break away from the group and head towards you. I warned JP, but he ignored me. He was concentrating on getting you out of there. You spotted Claude approaching. I heard you warning JP, *JP, someone's coming. Oh Christ, it's Claude; he's got a gun.'*"

Del continued, "And then I heard Claude yelling. *'You motherfucker; you're a dead man, JP'*". "Claude was pointing the gun at him. Claude yelled at you next. *'You too, you bitch. You wanna be with this white trash; you'll see him in hell.'*"

Del paused to take a drag. "I reached for the tire iron in the back seat and was running towards Claude when we heard the cop.

'Drop the gun boy!' the cop yelled. He was reaching for his weapon when Claude shot him. Claude started to turn towards JP, when you stabbed him in the side. You left the knife in him as he fell to the ground. You stood there horrified at what you had done. Claude was still moving. He was twitching on the ground, the gun still in his hand. I grabbed JP's arm and said—

He's still alive JP.*"

*'*JP turned to me *'Get her out of here. Del. Get her back to the projects. I'll take care of him. Come back and get me.'*

"You were in a daze. I took you to the projects. Edenwald was like a ghost town. All the gangbangers were down the Avenue. I dropped you off at your aunt's building. There were a couple of kids hangin' out front who knew you. They brought you inside.

"I went back to the school. JP was waiting in the shadows. He was carrying the knife. He jumped in the car and threw the knife in the glove compartment. Nothing was said. I didn't know he killed Claude at the time. I learned much later. We got to the Avenue, but it was over. We saw the police cars and ambulance. Everyone had split. A couple of days later, he asked me what I did with the knife. I told him I had gotten rid of it. It was never brought up again."

"When did he find out what really happened to my sister and uncle?"

"The next day; Contelmo came to him for advice. JP told him to forget about it. I asked him if he was going to tell you. He said you would be better off not knowing." Del pushed the envelope towards her.

She looked into his eyes. "The knife?"

"I don't know why I kept it. There are three sets of fingerprints on it: yours, JP's, and mine. Don't ask me how I know. But that's when I realized JP killed Claude. You were long gone by then. Do with it what you will, Tanya."

She took the envelope and pushed it into her bag. "I'm going to mail it to Lieutenant Mongelli. The incident will always be called self-defense, but the knife may bring the Lieutenant some closure.

"JP did Father Martin, Del. You know that?"

"I suspected it, Tanya. They'll find someone who saw him that day. He has to answer for that."

"He all ready has, Del. JP is not coming back. It's your company now. You paid your dues."

"Yeh, and I assume that JP finally paid his." He smiled and took her hand. "Let's have another drink. We both deserve it."

After saying his goodbyes, Del left the restaurant and entered the limo. As it pulled away from the curb, he noticed a small flock of pigeons sitting on the ledge above the restaurant entrance.

His thoughts went back to 1957. He remembered being on the roof of the five-story building where Satch resided. It was a beautiful, bright spring day. Even the sound of the Lexington Avenue Express a short distance away, brakes screeching as it entered the 225th Street Station, could not spoil the mood. They were removed from the street noises, the people, and the dirt of the Avenue.

He, JP, Terri, Annie, and Satch's latest love, Julie, were sitting on the roof ledge. They were sharing Genoa salami and provolone heroes and washing them down with a six-pack of Rheingold beer. They were watching Satch work his birds.

He let the sixty pigeons out of the coop and coaxed them into the air. His flock, containing a preponderance of homing pigeons mixed with tumblers and tipplers, soared high above the coop. Then as one, the flock took off into the blue.

The intention was to capture a pair of white Kings that strayed from their flock. These birds were fairly rare, and if Satch could coax them to join his birds, they would be worth some real money. Sure enough, the two Kings saw Satch's flock and joined them. He had them captured. Cupping his hands around his mouth, Satch started making cooing sounds, calling the pigeons home. The birds, hearing the call, started to make their way back to the coop.

Suddenly, high above the flock there was a screeching call. The pigeons started to dart about, trying to escape. A red-tailed hawk, high above, spotted the flock and its favorite target, the tumblers. Del remembered the moment vividly. The group was mesmerized by the hawk as it began its dive. The tumbler never had a chance, and they watched as the hawk grabbed the pigeon in its talons and flew off. Satch continued to call the birds, and finally retrieved all of them, except for the hawk's victim. A pall was cast over the small picnic on the roof. Satch said nothing for a minute and then mused aloud, but more to himself. "Not too bad, one tumbler for two white Kings. It was a good sacrifice."

Del sat back and closed his eyes as the limo made its way down Park Avenue. He smiled. At the end of the twenty-year conflict between Tanya and JP, Tanya turned out to be the red-tailed hawk, and JP, the tumbler.

What bookie on the Avenue would have taken that bet?

THE END